Princess

She's no ordinary princess.
Her hidden secrets are out of this world!

ROBIN PEDDIESON

PAGE PUBLISHING
Conneaut Lake, PA

First originally published by Page Publishing 2022

ISBN 978-1-6624-8524-4 (pbk)
ISBN 979-8-88654-362-9 (hc)
ISBN 978-1-6624-8527-5 (digital)

Printed in the United States of America

Chapter 1

What Was That?

It was an exceptionally beautiful day for my walk to work. Although my sneakers didn't exactly compliment my two-piece suit, they were so much more practical for walking than the heels that were tucked in the small tote that was hanging off my shoulder. As my destination became visible from a short distance away, I marveled at the sight of this noble red brick building. The tall white pillars that supported the expansive open entrance served to compliment this dignified and almost sacred place. This charming, vintage, but beautiful courthouse was filled to capacity, which wasn't surprising given that the focus of this case gained so much media attention. Cases involving abuse always attract so much interest. For some reason, people always like to assume that the victim is the one lying about the events that took place. The old-fashioned cast iron light fixtures that dimly lit the room confirmed that some faces were affable, but then there were those not so friendly looks cast my way as well. It was my job to show that the hours of my professional evaluation concerning this particular young lady demonstrated that she was of sound mind and had the capacity to distinguish right from wrong. Aside from the physical proof within her case, I needed to convey to the court that I not only found my client to be mentally sound but also she was as honest and truthful as any human being could possibly be.

My sweaty palms clutched the worn, wooden bench where I was seated as my heart pounded in my chest. I started to feel nauseous. As I blotted the perspiration from my forehead, I realized that the long blond hair covering the back of my neck was adding to the warm, stuffy atmosphere of the room. It's not like me to feel this jittery, but I usually don't have to wait so long to be called to the stand. Sitting here for over two hours already was contributing to my nervousness. What was different about this hearing? By all appearances, absolutely nothing was different. As I sat there, reminding myself that I am Sara Sanders, the expert witness called for such cases, I found that my confidence was beginning to return, and I looked forward to making my statement and answering any questions that might be asked. My turn to testify had to be nearing by now, so I pulled myself together and readied myself for the barrage of questions that I knew would be hurled at me.

I did, however, take comfort in the kind face of the presiding judge. While he dwarfed the huge antique desk on the raised platform where he was seated, he had the appearance of a kind, grandfatherly figure who was considerably more than just middle aged, and the weathered creases on his face gave him a look of wisdom and impeccable judgment. As his giant hand fumbled with the gavel, the wooden hammer looked as though it was just a miniature prop. His voice definitely did not match his physical appearance. It resonated softly when he spoke. It was apparent to me that he was much different than any of the judges presiding over the previous cases that I had been involved with. That eased my anxiety, somewhat.

I don't know what I was so afraid of. I had the reputation, the education in science and theory, and the skills to convey the facts. As a clinical psychologist, I had respected credentials, common sense, and above all a conscience that wouldn't consent to anything but honesty. As the hearing proceeded, I became more relaxed, and somehow my confidence, convictions, and expertise stood out during my testimony. I felt as though I came through like a champ. It was a great feeling indeed to know that I hadn't let anyone down, at least not today. I did anticipate that this case would not carry on beyond one more day of testimony and was nearing an end. Being strong-willed and good at my job, I couldn't allow myself room for mistakes, and I tried harder than anyone I know never to make any. I know that never making a mistake is an unrealistic view, but I always gave it my best shot.

Thankfully though, the day was over now, and all I could think about was going home to unwind. I knew that when I was organized enough to leave the courtroom, warm bodies and elbows would still be maneuvering to leave the crowded room. After arranging my brief-case, I made my way to the exit door of the courtroom. The clatter of my heels against the oak flooring seemed earsplitting, but it hardly compared to the sound they made against the old green marble floor awaiting me in the hall. The spacious wrap around corridors echoed every sound made. I almost made it to the door leading to busy, traffic-filled streets when quite unexpectedly, I felt an eerie familiar presence. It was then that I caught a glimpse of a shadowy figure off in the distance. Even though it felt familiar to me, an alarming sensation ran through me, and chills in my body let me know immediately that this was not a pleasant familiar encounter. This presence had a menacing darkness, and the feeling of terror that ran through my body was overwhelming, but I didn't know why. Even though this darkness was familiar, I have no recollection as to why it should be. After looking away and quickly glancing back, I saw nothing. It was there one minute and gone the next. Even with so many people moving about the room, it seemed as though I was the only one to see it. Was it there for only my benefit? It was undeniable yet inconceivable to me that any of this was real. I convinced myself that it was because of an unusually difficult week and this very long day that my mind was just playing tricks on me. What a strange day this has been. First, the unfamiliar feeling in the courtroom and now this! I just wanted this day to be over.

After this disturbingly hard day, a relaxing bubble bath, a good book, and a glass of wine were just what I needed. I even treated myself to a couple of aromatic lavender candles to complete the atmosphere I was trying to achieve. I wanted to lavish forever in this warm water filled with mounds of bubbles, but my body was now the consistency of a prune. As they say, all good things must come to an end.

Feeling refreshed and comfortable, I sat on my sofa and surrounded myself with cushy pillows. With book in hand and of course a much-needed glass of wine sitting beside me, I found that all was well with the world, or was it? Apparently, in my relaxed state, I must have dozed off for a while. My dozing off was much more than just a little while though. The tall burl carved grandfather clock that stood so proudly in the corner of my living room woke me when it echoed out three chimes. Could it possibly be 3:00 a.m. already? I think I was dreaming, but after retracing the events of my dream, I found them to be fragmented and incomplete, not to mention a tad bit disturbing. I again found my brain convincing the logical part of me that it was just a dream. After realizing that I definitely did dream, the parts that I could remember, although foggy, were too impossible to be real. It didn't seem like a normal dream that even my subconscious mind would have experienced. That same feeling of dread was again taking over my body. As I reached for my wine, my hand shook, and my body was quivering so much so that a couple of droplets spilled over as I tried to bring the glass to my lips. After gulping down the final warming remainder of my wine, I took a deep breath and tried to make sense out of this bizarre dream. A dream that I remember having yet one I could hardly remember.

I kept trying to make sense of the senseless, but I just couldn't, so I directed my thoughts elsewhere. Now, being wide awake, I went back to reading and stuck with it for quite a while until I realized that I had read the same page over and over, still not understanding what I had read. Reading now was completely pointless. The hour was indeed late, so I decided that I might as well go to bed and try to sleep. What an unusual night this has been.

Chapter 2

What a Night

Well, today is a new day, and I feel sapped of energy! I wondered if I got any sleep at all last night. As my feet hit the floor, I felt wobbly and a bit unsteady. My bed revealed evidence of some serious tossing and turning as well. Blankets were in a pile, the pillows were thrown here and there, and my beautiful floral bedspread was lying in a heap on the floor. I don't remember my sleep as having been fitful, but the evidence was there. It actually brought back memories of my college days and looked as though I had thrown a party. In reality, I knew that my having a party was a ridiculous thought.

Knowing that I had another full day ahead of me, I went directly to the bathroom to shower and get ready for work. As I meandered slowly past the mirror, I had to do a double take. You know, it was one of those quick glances that pulls you back for a longer look. That couldn't possibly be me, could it? I looked as if I had wrestled an alligator, and worse yet, I felt like it too. My body was achy, and even more curiously, I had some minor bruises to prove it too. What the hell happened? Did I walk in my sleep? Did I fall down a flight of stairs? Do I have some kind of split personality that I'm unaware of? Oh, so many unanswered questions. Maybe I just might need an extended vacation in the tranquility of a tropical paradise somewhere. It seems as though my usually normal, uneventful life has suddenly become anything but normal or uneventful.

This was one of those mornings that I definitely needed coffee first, lots of coffee! Closing my eyes, I savored that heavenly aroma as it brewed and then that wonderful first sip. I knew that I would enjoy every cup. As I sat there enjoying my momentary peace, I suddenly felt uneasy yet again, and something told me that leaving my apartment just might be a mistake, but I had no choice in the matter. My testimony today was imperative, and I had to resist my inner instinct. I knew that my testimony today could put an end to this case that I had put so much time and effort into. I was completely committed but extremely grateful that the docket was set for later in the day. It gave me some much-needed time to relax and mentally prepare for the hopefully climactic day this would be.

As I had hoped, this monumental case had come to an end within a couple of hours and ended well for my client. After all the hugging and appreciation for my efforts was expressed, I was relieved to know that I had played a part in bringing closure to the painful experience of such a beautiful young lady. Once again, I knew that I had the ability to impact another life in a positive way.

I was feeling pretty full of myself when I left the courtroom. Wearing the smile of gratification on my face and walking to the beat of my own drum, my breath was taken away as I encountered that dark, shadowy figure once again. He—and I'm only assuming that it was a he—was always too far off in the distance for me to see absolute features. I think he is an adult man, but I just can't be sure. I thought I caught a brief glimpse of a profile, but it didn't resemble a man's profile. Actually, it didn't resemble a familiar profile at all. I do remember thinking that he must be a total coward though, always keeping his distance and then disappearing as quickly as he appeared. Was I being watched? Of course, as before, the thought of my mind playing tricks on me was present. I kept thinking about the day before, the sleep-filled but extremely restless night, the bruises on my body, and now this! The pieces of this extraordinary puzzle are just too few to put together right now.

However, knowing me as I do and being the mover and shaker that I am, I feel confident that somehow I will figure it all out. With the hearing completed and feeling reassured by the outcome, I can now take some time off. Being financially secure allows me the privilege of playing hooky for a while, and I'm really looking forward to some R&R without incident.

I'm not sure what I will be doing during that time, but I know that a tropical vacation right now is out of the question. I know that I won't be able to sit around, doing nothing for very long. Being lost in thought and weighing my different options while walking home, I found myself a good city block past my apartment entrance. Looking like an idiot, I stood there laughing out loud at my very unusual lack of attention to detail. As I turned to retrace my footsteps back to my apartment, it became more apparent than ever that I needed some rest and resting was number one on my new bucket list. Well, that didn't last long. Rest would now become number two on my bucket list. I bumped into an old familiar friend on the way back. We haven't seen each other in at least two years, so stopping for a bite of dinner along with a cocktail or two seemed like the best idea ever. Margie's appearance hadn't changed a bit. She was tall, slender, and still very attractive, about two inches taller than me and brunette. I've always been drawn to her hands though. Her long narrow fingers were always so graceful and beautiful. In my mind, I could see why any man would find them to be sensual. But like me, she was unmarried and dedicated her life to her work. I can understand why being a chemist would be demanding. Heading her department, she is an inspiration to her team, and their research has proven to be of great value. We had a wonderful time talking about earlier years and just catching up with the current events of our lives. Then our reminiscing took us as far back as our high school years. Oh, how cruel hindsight can be at times! We thought we were so smart, and of course, we thought we knew everything. Yes, we had all the answers. We both started laughing at our innocent stupidity and decided that we should call it a night. We vowed to never again allow two years to pass without keeping in touch. I don't know why, but for some strange reason, I had the feeling that keeping in touch wasn't in the cards for us. It was a lovely idea though, and I loved the thought. I put it out of my mind and wore a smile on my face all the way home.

Chapter 3

More Confusion and a Little OCD

Making it back to that old brownstone building that I inhabit and after exchanging pleasantries with my neighbor Stan, I continued on to my second-floor apartment and slid the key into the lock on my door. I was startled when the door opened without the need of my assistance. I was both surprised and disturbed all at the same time. I am certain that I locked my door when I left earlier that afternoon. I'm not a careless person, and I have a routine that I follow. I started running the routine through my mind—turn off the lights, check the thermostat for the proper temperature, double check to see that the coffee pot is off, and, above all, make sure I have my purse and briefcase and then walk out of the door and lock it. It's a habit.

Stan started to enter his apartment just across the hall from mine, but seeing that I appeared to be slightly shaken, he asked if I was all right. I told him what had happened, and being the friend and gentleman that he was, he offered to accompany me inside. I was relieved that I had someone to survey the dark corners for me on this somewhat scary tour. Everything seemed to be in place, and nothing was missing. After he checked the closets and every other nook and cranny, we found that there was nothing out of place or out of the ordinary and I didn't have any unwelcome visitors lurking about. I gave him my profound thanks and offered him a nightcap. I didn't have a lot of close friends, but we've been good friends for a long time now. Most of the friends that I had growing up were scattered all over the globe, and we barely kept in touch if at all. I didn't have much time for the social media thing, but every once in a while, I would take a peek to see if any posts were recognizable to me. Stan and I had gone to dinner a couple of times and enjoyed the company of each other immensely. But having few things in common, we drifted in the direction of keeping our relationship platonic. Since then, our friendship has blossomed. He's free to call on me at any time, and I can call on him just as I had tonight. He declined my offer of a nightcap though as he was facing an early morning appointment and looked forward to unwinding and getting some sleep.

I can't say that I was upset by his denying me the pleasure of his company. All I wanted to do was take my work clothes off and get comfortable. I slid the heels off my screaming feet and then proceeded to make the rest of me as comfortable as my newly released feet were. And having a slight case of OCD, I made sure that my clothes were neat and orderly, hanging in their proper place, and any clothes needing to be laundered were properly thrown with a carefree abandon into the hamper. With my second shower of the day behind me and now in the comfort of cozy pajamas and slippers, I poured a glass of wine and sat down to read at least one chapter of the book that I started two weeks earlier. It usually doesn't take me very long to read a book, especially if it completely grabs my attention and I'm really into it. I have a variety of interests when it comes to reading, but I find romance novels to be so relaxing. They always seem to take me to places that I've never explored, and even though most are fiction, as in real life, I find the elements of their relationships to be very complicated and often problematic. It seems as though this book was going to be the exception though. Somehow, I think the forces are working against me, and I'm not meant to finish it. I didn't realize how completely exhausted I was until I sat down. I sat there for a minute or two sipping my wine and trying to concentrate on reading, but somehow, the pages wouldn't come into focus. I gave in to my fatigue and determined that reading wouldn't be a good idea.

I would probably have to reread everything that I had read over and over, just like the night before.

The comfort of my bed was calling to me, and I couldn't refuse its summons as I could hardly keep my eyes open. I drifted off into sweet slumber within minutes. The activity of my nonstop thinking wouldn't be keeping me awake tonight. It was my absolute pleasure to drift off so quickly and actually stay asleep. Morning arrived with the warmth of the sun peaking through the blinds. Morning has always been my favorite part of the day, but reflecting on the perfect night's sleep, I found it a little peculiar that I was still so tired. I felt certain that my sleep was undisturbed. I can't say for sure, but my gut was telling me that something was off, and my intuition seemed heightened and intense. I've learned to trust my gut because it's rarely wrong, and if my intuition tells me to pay attention, I pay attention. My sixth sense told me that my dream cycle was long and lasted throughout the entire night. This dream seemed to feel not only so much more real and so much more vivid than usual but also much more elusive. I didn't have my usual total recall. Hell, I didn't even have fragmented recall. Yet somehow, I knew that I had dreamed. That in itself was so strange and so out of the ordinary. With my inability to remember the context, I didn't have any way of knowing if they were harmless dreams or dreams that I should be concerned about. I was perplexed by my lack of recollection, but I do know for certain that I did dream all the way through the entire night. I don't think I've ever had a dream last that long. Why can't I remember? This makes no sense to me at all. I usually had funny dreams or bizarre dreams related to work or totally nonsensical dreams, but I could always remember them. Now, I remember nothing. Oh well, I could lay here forever and drive myself crazy, but what's the point? I was craving that wonderful morning cocktail called coffee, and it was time to plan my day. When I swung my legs over the side of the bed to stand up, they gave way beneath me and resisted supporting the usual weight of my body. I immediately found myself resting on the floor. I was unhurt but startled all the same. What is happening to me? I looked around the room as if I expected someone to have seen this klutzy stunt. I smiled and was sure glad that I lived alone because

I must have been a sight to see. Even I was tempted to laugh. As I was pulling myself up, leaning on the bed, I couldn't help but notice that my back was tender, but at least my sea legs were gone and I was grateful for that. Now I'm beginning to be a little concerned, but I refuse to give in to my confusion, and I will not let it get in the way of my time off work. Not giving it any more thought for now, I made my way into the kitchen to make a pot of coffee, which I intended to drink in its entirety. The familiar aroma was just divine, and today I could linger in luxury for as long as I wanted to because I didn't have anywhere special to be and I didn't have any appointments to keep. That's such a welcome feeling for a change.

Chapter 4

--- ❧ ---

A Full Heart

Having time off gave me the opportunity to attend to some things that I had been avoiding for far too long. Going through old photos and organizing them always seemed like a monumental task, so that seemed to be a good place to start. I don't know why I avoided it for so long. I actually found that I was enjoying every minute. Sorting through old photos and placing them into the awaiting empty albums that I had purchased so long ago turned into a most pleasurable task. Every photograph that I touched filled my heart with so many wonderful memories. Some even caused a tear or two to slip down my cheeks, especially the ones of my folks. My dad loved golfing, and so did mom, but her real passion was photography. She loved taking pictures of nature's landscapes and animals. There were so many here in my collection. Some of them were extraordinary and deserving of a frame and of a place to proudly be displayed. I'm sure I can find a suitable shelf to exhibit them. If I don't find a place for all of them at home, then perhaps I'll put some in my office to be enjoyed by everyone. My mom and dad were such special people to me and were the most important people in my world. I don't remember them being anything but loving and kind. I think that those qualities are fixed in my mind because I was adopted. I wasn't an infant when I was adopted, so naturally, being older allowed me the time to hear all the gruesome stories of adopted kids and how mistreated they always were by their adoptive parents. Of course, it didn't take long for me to realize that there was absolutely no truth in those stories. Nothing could have been farther from the truth. Having so many reminders of their love just sitting here in front of me, I feel a peace in my heart that I haven't felt in a long while.

Among the old photos, I found some paperwork and certificates from school, and of course, my mom kept everything else that I had made for them throughout my school years. My parents knew that I was an exceptional student but didn't force me to take classes beyond my capabilities. They left that for me to decide. As it turned out, I did choose to take the classes that my teachers and advisors encouraged me to take, most of which were for gifted children. I did well and excelled throughout my school years, even in college. Mixed among the certificates, tucked inside a file folder, was a folded certificate that I hadn't seen before. Much to my surprise, I discovered that it was my birth certificate. When I opened it, I found it odd that the vast majority of the pertinent information had been redacted. Why was so much information hidden? I never did have a desire to seek out my birth parents. I didn't in my youth and I don't now, but I still found it to be out of the ordinary. I knew that this discovery would play on my mind for a while, but I convinced myself to put it away and move on to whatever came next. I folded it back up and placed it back into the folder and kept it among all of the other certificates and papers. My trip down memory lane led me to relatives on my mother's side of the family. My Aunt Ellen, who was the total opposite of my mom and even of her own husband, Uncle Tom, graced me with a few mug shots. She definitely wasn't my favorite person. Unfortunately, Uncle Tom never found his own voice. I wish he had though because his deep tone would have been heard over Aunt Ellen's. It was obvious that Aunt Ellen was the boss! On occasion, usually on a holiday, we would get together for a celebration. As I recall, it was never much of a celebration though. Aunt Ellen was the rule maker and the disciplinarian, and Uncle Tom just went along with her, I suppose because he was so passive and it was easier than confronting her. She always seemed to be angry at the world and took it out on my cousin, Jenny.

If an outsider had to guess which one of us was the adopted child, I feel quite certain that Jenny would have been chosen. I felt so bad for her, and she knew it, but it made us love each other all that much more. We loved spending time together, and being only a year apart in age, we got on very well and shared many of the same interests. I tried to make sure that Jenny experienced as much fun as possible during their visits. She had a right to be happy, at least for the short time that we were together. I always let her pick what game we would play. Most of the time, she just wanted to sit quietly and talk. I was absolutely fine with that. Those times created such precious memories of her. It was during those discussions that I realized the full extent of her miserable life. The sadness in her glistening eyes said more than any words she might say. I always felt my own sadness when they left to go home. I knew the kind of life that Jenny was facing, and the thought was almost more than I could bear. During one of their visits, I remember my mum trying to convince my aunt to let Jenny stay with us for an extended vacation, but she wouldn't hear of it. She knew that Jenny would never want to go home. They lived so far away, and Jenny wasn't even allowed to use the telephone. She was allowed to write to me occasionally, and by occasionally, I mean a couple of times a year. Needless to say, when she reached legal age, she left her parents' home for some unknown destination. Because they were so cold and strict, she never felt the same loving intimacy and warmth from her parents as I did from mine. The people that touch our lives can leave marks on our hearts and souls that last a lifetime. I fear that Jenny's marks are like wounds that bleed leaving scars behind. She wanted nothing to do with them, and I couldn't blame her. She did write to me a couple of times to let me know that all was good and that she was fine and doing well. There was never a return address, and the postmark on the envelope was always too blurry to see where it had come from. I could only hope that the marks I left on her heart would make her smile with the same affection for me as I had for her. The dreams that young girls have while growing up seldom become reality. Hopefully, Jenny's dreams of escaping and living happily and, most of all, of being loved became her reality. I don't know anyone who deserves it more.

The memories that I have of my own mom and dad are all good and make my heart happy. Oh sure, I could be a typical kid, and I did disobey them a couple of times, but the punishment always fit the crime, and I knew that I deserved their very appropriate retribution. They always seemed so wise and successfully prepared me for adulthood, the good as well as the bad. They paved a path that equipped me to pursue my dreams of having a successful career and made sure that I knew how to rely on myself. I'm happy and well adjusted, and I love the world around me. Unfortunately, I can't share my successes or failures with them. Sadly, my dad died of a fatal heart attack, and I think my mom missed him so much that she died of a broken heart only a couple of years later. It's impossible for a daughter to replace the love and companionship that was shared between them for so many years. I miss them both so very much. I finished getting the photo albums together and just sat there feeling a sense of accomplishment and was lost inside my own thoughts. All in all, I considered it to be an enjoyable, worthwhile day. I could hardly believe the time, but my stomach was complaining that I hadn't taken the time to eat all day. Since I hadn't planned on doing any actual cooking, I ordered take out. After all, I was on vacation, sort of. I hadn't had Italian food in a very long time and decided that it would blend wonderfully with a beautiful red wine that was waiting to be opened and enjoyed. It was just begging to be opened. I more than enjoyed this marvelous meal and, much to my disappointment, had no leftovers for the following day. I remember thinking that it was for the best anyway because I don't usually indulge in such extravagant, calorie-laden food. I hate to admit it, but I knew that it was just a matter of time before staying slim in figure wouldn't be quite as easy as it had been up until now.

Before I knew it, darkness had drifted in just as that ominous dark shadow had done yesterday. The evening darkness wasn't exactly unwelcome because that was usually my true alone time for relaxing. I think I enjoyed those few early hours of darkness almost as much as early morning. The wind was picking up, and the weather report predicted possible rain on and off throughout the night. What a great night to stay in, watch a little TV, and perhaps read. The red wine that accompanied my dinner so nicely was sitting there, waiting to be poured into my second glass. It was a spectacular recipe for a peaceful, quiet evening.

Chapter 5

The Trip

As midnight ushered its way in, I found that I was actually exhausted, and my eyelids were so heavy. Although not a strenuous day, it was an emotional full day of silent activity, and I was entirely relaxed and ready to call it a night. After going through my usual evening routine, much like when I leave for work in the morning, I carefully folded the covers back and climbed into the most comfortable bed I have ever owned.

Although I found it difficult to get into a comfortable position, I quickly fell into a deep sleep. However, my sleep was interrupted, and I found myself laying there wide awake at 3:00 a.m. What is it about 3:00 a.m.? My internal clock must need resetting. I tried going back to sleep but found it impossible. The only light illuminating the room came from the moon peering through small cracks between the slats of the blinds. I couldn't lie there indefinitely, staring at a barely visible ceiling. I got out of bed and made myself comfortable on the sofa with my book and of course another glass of wine. Maybe reading would make me drowsy. In my haste to resume my reading, I didn't even take time to put my robe and slippers on. After situating myself on the sofa, I grabbed the afghan that was neatly folded nearby and covered my body pretty much up to my chin with just my arms hanging out. I wasn't pretty, but I was very comfortable. I sat there engrossed in the best romance novel that I had the pleasure of reading in a very long time. Before I knew it, I was starting the last chapter and was anticipating a very juicy and passionate conclusion. I reached for my wine, took a lingering sip, and set the glass back on the side table. Looking back to the last paragraph where I left off, I realized that something didn't seem right. I was suddenly alarmed by my imagination playing such cruel tricks on me again. In an effort to be certain that I wasn't losing my mind, I peeked back at my wine glass. The table that my wine glass was sitting on wasn't my table. How can that be? That's not my table! I looked a second time, and I wasn't mistaken; this was definitely not my table. Looking at my surroundings, I found that I was no longer sitting on my sofa, but instead, I was sitting upright in a very comfortable red wing back chair, still in my pajamas with the afghan wrapped around me and book in hand. My back seemed to be slightly more sore than it had been, so I wasn't leaning all the way back. At that very moment, although my eyes never left my book, I felt knifelike piercing eyes fixed on me. They were definitely the eyes of inquisition, probably because they couldn't believe what they were seeing any more than I could.

My entire being appeared to be opaque and somewhat faded. Eventually, I came into focus, but by all appearances, I looked something like a hologram for a few seconds. I know that describing it like that is bizarre, but I don't know of a better description. How crazy is that? If something like that showed up out of nowhere in my living room, my reaction would be indescribable, I'm sure! Finally, I felt like myself, back in my whole body with a racing heart and rapid breathing. In my shock and bewilderment, I was afraid to take my eyes totally off my book, but my peripheral vision gave me just enough information to let me know that this entire experience was extraordinarily abnormal and more than a little strange. I felt a little disorientated and just sat there holding my book. It was a hard cover book, so in my mind, it would become my savior if necessary. I've never used a book as a weapon before, but there's always a first time for everything! My mind was racing, and I think I was in that fight-or-flight state that I've heard people speak of. I finally rallied the courage to look up. The book that my fingers were so tightly gripping flew into the air. I jumped out of the chair and tried to hide behind it as if being two feet farther away would put me in a safe space. My wine glass was still sitting on the side table, and not a single drop had been spilled. Thank God for that because I really needed it now. Slowly inching my hand toward the glass, my eyes were set and didn't move from the two men who were staring at me. Carefully pulling the glass toward me, I picked it up and guzzled the last of it, which, by the way, was a considerable amount. Damn, I wish there had been more though! I was afraid to speak and kept waiting for one or both of them to explain how I got there and more importantly why. I can't explain it now. but for some reason, it felt as though I was standing in the apartment of the tallest man of the two. I have no idea as to why I felt that way or how I knew that, but I would have confirmation of that later on.

This staring match went on for what seemed like forever. and the silence was deafening. At first, I was too stunned to speak and kept waiting for them to make the first move. Due to their silence, and being of the female persuasion with an insatiable curiosity engrained in me, I could resist no longer. I needed to find out what the hell just happened. That "mover and shaker" part of me finally managed to initiate a strained conversation. I am basically a shy person, but I'm a pretty strong person so I just had to put myself out there to get the ball rolling. Somehow, I managed to sheepishly cough out a question. "What are your names?" The tallest of the men said, "My name is Sean Murphy," and then he introduced the other man as his best friend, Liam Doyle. Sean was tall with wavy strawberry blond hair and a stubbly kind of beard that is so popular today and very easy on the eyes. Liam was a brunette, perhaps two or so inches shorter than Sean, clean shaven, and also a very nicely put together man. None of that mattered now, but with so many thoughts running around in my head, I supposed that since I was literally picked up and dropped into a strange place, this was better than so many places I could think of. After all, I could be finding myself smack-dab in the middle of the city dump! Still, this was all so unsettling. I continued on with my interrogation because I had so many questions. I went on with my follow-up question. "How did you bring me here, and why did you bring me here?" They looked at each other and then back at me as if I had two heads! With a quivering voice, Sean said, "What do you mean how did we bring you here and why? We thought that you might be able to tell us how you got here and why?"

That conversation didn't go well, and it certainly wasn't the answer I was looking for. It seems that the answer to that question would evade us all for some time to come. They did, however, manage to ask me what my name was. I immediately started to answer and said, "My name is…my name is…Oh God, I don't even know what my name is!" Why don't I know what my name is? I knew what it was yesterday! I'm absolutely sure of that. Finding this to be really scary and upsetting, my eyes began to well up with tears. I'm not usually a crier, but at the time, it seemed appropriate for the position I was in. I had to reassure myself that under these circumstances, I was entitled to cry. I looked away from them because I didn't want to appear to be weak. I quickly wiped the tears away, regained my composure, and turned back to meet them straight on, eye to eye. I decidedly moved a bit forward toward them in a threatening way, like a soldier going into battle. I was anxious to redeem myself, so in the most demanding voice I could muster, I said, "Look at me! Just look at me. Do you honestly believe that I do my traveling wearing pajamas with an afghan wrapped around me carrying my own glass of wine to the party?" At that, they both smiled and began snickering like two undisciplined school boys. I found no humor in it whatsoever, and again, my eyes were welling with unstoppable tears, so I turned away from them and walked over to a dining room chair in the adjoining room. After placing my hands on the back of the chair, I slightly hung my head and quietly cried. It was the only thing I could do at that point. I wasn't giving up mind you; I was just having an unavoidable breakdown. I didn't bring myself here, and they didn't seem to have any special powers to bring me here, so how the hell did I get here? I found myself wondering if the shadow figure that I had seen earlier could possibly have some kind of connection, or was that just some weird coincidence? I was so overwhelmed I found it impossible to think rationally.

Seeing that I was an emotional wreck, Sean walked over and tried to comfort me. He placed his hands on my shoulders, making me immediately arch my back. I felt an excruciating pain that I didn't even know existed until that exact moment. Sean quickly released me and asked if he startled me or if touching me had caused pain. What else could possibly cause that kind of reaction? I told him I wasn't in the mood to pretend, so yes that really did hurt a lot. As politely as he could, he asked if he could have a look. At first, I thought he had some morbid need to satisfy his own curiosity, but I soon learned that he was honestly concerned for me. I told him to go ahead and take a look. I certainly couldn't see it from my vantage point, and I wasn't at all sure that I wanted to just then anyway. Oh, the crazy thoughts we have when we are in an extremely stressful situation. I couldn't help but reflect on the fact that we just met about forty-five minutes ago and already this man is lifting up the back of my pajama top! As he pulled it up slowly and as gently as possible, I did feel some relief to have the fabric lifted away from my skin.

In his astonishment, he let out a gasp of disbelief and motioned for Liam to take a look. I knew it was picture-worthy when I heard the click of a cell phone camera. They couldn't believe their eyes or what they were actually looking at. Sean didn't want to make me stand in that somewhat embarrassing position any longer than necessary. As gently as possible, he lowered my top. Even though I was hurting, I couldn't imagine that it was all that bad. But according to their reaction, it must have looked like I did wrestle that alligator after all. Before pursuing further conversation, Sean, in the most caring way, said, "Before we talk about or do another thing, I'm going to take care of this!" While he was tending to the mysterious wounds on my back, he said that he didn't have imagination enough to even guess what could have happened to me. He told me that whoever had done this was filled with an enormous amount of rage. As he was thinking out loud, under his breath, he said that this is far beyond a normal human being's comprehension. He had a burning need to know how something this severe could have happened without my knowing about it or having a clue as to how it happened and why. Once again, I couldn't stop the tears from flowing as I whispered

that I knew there was no logic in it, but I really didn't have any recollection of anything happening to me or how something this severe
could happen without my knowing who, when, where, or why. I
don't know how that could possibly be, but it's the God's honest
truth.

We were all tired and emotionally exhausted, worn out, confused, and too many other adjectives to mention, but I needed the
answer to one last question. I had to know exactly where I was.
Judging from the heavy accent of the two men, either they were new
to the United States, or I wasn't in Kansas anymore, just a figure of
speech of course. Either way, I had to know. Sean said, "You're in my
apartment, in County Cork, in the country of Ireland."

I just stared at him and then blurted out, "What? Ireland?"
How can that be? I kept thinking to myself that it was impossible,
yet here I was. That was some trip considering I wasn't buzzed and
I have never done drugs! Under the circumstances, Sean and Liam
were warm and welcoming beyond any expectations that I might
have. Due to my emotional and physical condition, Sean said he
would let me stay in his guest room for the night and that we would
try to sort everything out in the morning. Since I didn't even know
where I was, it was obvious that I had nowhere else to go. I was
totally helpless. I'm not sure that I would have been that welcoming
of a stranger if he or she popped up out of nowhere in my apartment,
but I was ever so grateful that Sean was or I surely would have been
stranded on the street.

Chapter 6

If Only to Sleep

I splashed cool water on my swollen eyes, hoping to make my crying less noticeable, but I can't say that it helped much. Hopefully by morning, I would look more like a human. I could only hope.

Even though seeing my entire back was impossible, I took a peak at it in the bedroom mirror. I was appalled by the condition of the small portion of my back that was visible to me. I could see that healing and getting back to normal was going to take more than just a few days. There were huge, raised black and blue bruises, accompanied by cuts, scrapes, and other marks that can only be described as some kind of artwork or design that filled every visible inch of space on my back. My breath was taken away at the sight of my mutilated body. I couldn't stop asking myself why and who would do something this awful to me and the more obvious question, why don't I remember any of it? I'm sure that there could be people out there in this world that aren't fond of me but this? I can't imagine anyone hating me that much. Lying on my back in bed was definitely out of the question, so I picked my most comfortable side. I was so exhausted and ready for sleep, but I didn't have an on and off button for my brain. My thoughts just won't stop, and I'm feeling totally troubled where Sean and Liam are concerned. They have been wonderful, but I can't imagine that they would want to be involved in this insanity.

Why should they be, and why would they even consider it? What am I going to do? I found myself whispering a prayer, asking God to please help me unravel this mystery and to let me close my eyes and sleep, even if only for a little while.

I had a hard time sleeping, and the night seemed so long. Morning was elusive as the hours of darkness seemed endless. I'm not sure exactly when I fell asleep, but I do know that it was a short, restless sleep. I could barely focus my eyes when I woke up. I looked over at the clock, and the blurred numbers were showing the time to be 11:00 a.m. I was surprised to see that it was late morning, but Sean thought that I needed the rest, so he didn't disturb me. He wanted to let me sleep as long as possible due to the events of the prior evening. Liam went back to his own apartment the night I arrived but told Sean that he would be back in the morning. Liam had returned as promised and was waiting with Sean for me to get up. As I staggered out into the kitchen, I must have been a sight to behold. I could tell by the look on their faces when I walked into the room that my rough night was obvious. I had been so preoccupied with so many indistinct thoughts I hadn't bothered to look at myself in the mirror. They would probably have laughed if my appearance hadn't been so serious. Sean said that if I wanted to borrow a brush or comb, it was no problem, but apologized for not having an extra toothbrush. He said, "You'll find a comb and brush in the drawer of the vanity." I shuffled down the hall and made my way to the bathroom to see if I really looked that bad. Oh, Lord! I was scary beyond words. I would have laughed myself if I had been there under different circumstances. I pulled my hair back into a ponytail and tried to look at least presentable until I could shower. I hoped that Sean would let me use his shower. Sean made a second pot of coffee and offered me a fresh cup and breakfast as well, but I couldn't eat. All I wanted was coffee and some answers, but I was way past confusion about my situation. They very kindly let me sit there in silence while I sipped from the huge, heavy blue mug. After a while, words started pouring out of my mouth. "I don't know what's going to happen to me! I don't remember my name! How can I go back home when I don't know where home is? I have no personal items with me and obviously no clothes!" I was overwhelming myself with all of the details that were so urgently important to me. It was then that I realized that I needed to get control of my emotions. I told Sean and Liam that they were in no way responsible for me. This is my problem, not theirs! I think I was secretly afraid that they would want to totally bow out of this mess, but nonetheless, I made it clear that they were not expected to look after me. I'm not a friend, a relative, or even just an acquaintance. I'm a total stranger, and they have no obligation to provide me with the necessities of life. I could never ask them to, but having no place to call my own and no way to provide for myself was the most terrifying thought I've ever had. I would have been relieved if Sean offered to let me stay there while I sorted this mess out, but I couldn't count on it. I did see a kindness, or maybe it was a sadness in their eyes that made me feel as though they weren't going to flat out abandon me. A very short time later, Sean verbalized that very thought. I was so relieved to know that I wouldn't be abandoned. To say that I was grateful and appreciative is an understatement and completely inadequate. I felt as if I could relax and breathe a little. We all shared the same confusions and didn't know just where to start. I would say at the beginning, but what was the beginning?

Since I was the person of interest here, I supposed that it was up to me to initiate some kind of conversation. We all felt uncomfortable pursuing something that none of us knew anything about. How do we discuss the subject of something when we don't know exactly what the subject is? I thought for a minute and couldn't find a way to start a conversation about my randomly appearing here in Ireland. I couldn't share all of my thoughts with them because I myself found them to be far-fetched and unbelievable. We had already asked the same questions that didn't seem to have any apparent answers right at that moment. So the next best thing for now was to learn as much as we could about each other. In some ways, it seemed like we were just engaging in small talk, but information is what I really needed. I had to know more about them to help me sort this out. How did they tie into my new reality? Were they supposed to play a significant part? Those were the thoughts that were bouncing around in my head. Sean and Liam couldn't ask me about my life because I didn't even know my own name. I did remember most things not related to my identity though. Unfortunately, they seemed to be insignificant things that didn't put me any closer to knowing who I was or where I came from. I knew that I didn't have a husband or children, and I knew that my parents had both passed on. I knew that I had a few friends, but I didn't know who they were. I knew that I had a successful career, but what was that career? I didn't have a clue as to what I did for a living. I filled Sean and Liam in on those details, and they were glad to know at least that much about me, but the really important details were more than just out of reach; they seemed to be totally buried somewhere. If I knew even the smallest detail or even just one friend's name, I'd at least have a place to start. Even though I didn't know who I was or where I came from, knowing just one full name could possibly launch my investigation.

I asked Sean to tell me about himself. He seemed to be a little more shy than Liam and was the reserved type. He looked as though he was uncomfortable talking about himself and being in the spotlight. Judging from the way he kept repositioning himself in his chair, I knew that I was right. I touched the top of his arm and told him that I really needed to know about him. Knowing about Sean and Liam might help me to figure out how they fit into the grand scheme of things. At least, that's what I hoped. I pointed out that I already knew that he was a very gentle, kind man. I said, "Just look around this table, Sean. You have welcomed a perfect stranger into your home. You've tended to a stranger's wounds, and you've provided a comfortable place for this stranger to rest her head. Now I'd like to hear your story. Please tell me about you." I told Sean that he could start with the condensed version at any point in his life that he was comfortable with. Liam piped in and said that he would be glad to tell me everything about Sean and asked what I'd really like to know. After all, he knew Sean better than almost anybody. In his embarrassment, Sean's cheeks turned red, and he told Liam to sit there and be quiet. He then looked at me and told me not to believe a word of whatever Liam said. He had a vivid imagination and just makes up the story as he goes along. Nobody ever takes him seriously. I said, "Okay, if you don't want me to listen to Liam, then you're going to have to tell me your story." He seemed to have a difficult time getting started, so I looked at Liam and said, "It looks like you're going to have to get things started here. Tell me all about Sean."

Liam started out, "Well, you see, there was this one time, a few years back when we were younger and really brave..." Sean jumped in and told me once again to pay no attention to Liam because he always makes everything up and he doesn't really know what he's talking about anyway. Not wanting to push my luck, I asked Sean how old he was. He was quick to answer, and the number thirty slipped out of his mouth. I wanted to keep asking specific questions, but every now and then, my own situation crept back into my thoughts, and I wondered to myself, what am I doing here? It was hard not to be distracted by my own issues. I should be focusing on myself so that I don't have to impose further on Sean and his good nature. Nevertheless, I clumsily continued with my interrogation. "What do you do for a living Sean?"

Much to my surprise, he told me that he was a .NET developer. I did have some notion of what a .NET developer was, but I asked him to tell me exactly what the duties of a .NET developer were. At that point, I could see that Sean was feeling more at ease. A proud man views his profession as the defining feature of who he really is, so when he puffed up his chest, I knew that the ice had been broken. Sean told me that a .NET developer created online software and applications using the .NET framework and language. Now I'm telling myself that I know absolutely nothing about this .NET developer job. Sean continued to say that at times, a .NET developer would be expected to update existing software and provide technical support, and at other times, he would create applications to help solve issues or improve customer experience by writing code or fixing bugs. Feeling satisfied with himself, he leaned back in his chair and clasping his hands behind his head said, "That pretty much covers it." I was curious though. Today was a weekday. Why wasn't he at work? As it turns out, he has a home office and does much of his work from home although he is required to physically show up at his client's office on occasion.

Now it was Liam's turn. I asked Liam to tell me about himself, but before he could utter a word, Sean broke in and said, "Let me tell you all about Liam. Where he is concerned, there is some really juicy stuff that you might be interested in."

While I assured them both that I wanted to know everything, those stories would have to be told at a later date. Right now, I was basically interested in their everyday lives. I looked in Liam's direction and said, "So Liam, tell me, how old you are, and what you do for a living?" Liam was more than happy to fill in some details about himself and proceeded to tell me that he was also thirty years old and is a marketing consultant. I wasn't about to make the same mistake as I did with Sean, thinking that I already knew what a marketing consultant's duties were, so of course, I asked Liam to describe his job.

"Well now, you see," he started.

And Sean blurted out, "Cut the crap and get to it you, big phony."

Liam laughed and said, "All right, all right, all right! As a marketing consultant, I usually study a company's profile and operations in order to understand what their true marketing needs are. Then it's necessary for me to research and identify industry trends, and finally, when all is said and done, I develop and implement a marketing strategy according to objectives and budget. That's pretty much it in a nutshell."

I tried searching the depths of my brain to come up with a little something about myself, but it was impossible. How could all of my important memories be missing? Where did they go? I remember that I like steak, potatoes, pasta, chocolate, and other insignificant things, and I definitely remember what kind of wine I like. I remember what toothpaste I prefer and my favorite bodywash. Now, if I could only remember my own name. I couldn't help but wonder if this situation was permanent or just a temporary glitch in my life. The thought of it possibly being permanent was more than I could take in.

Trying not to show the disappointment in myself that I was feeling, I asked for another cup of coffee. By now, I was feeling that I might be able to eat a little something, and Sean offered to toast a crumpet for me. He let me know that he was in no way a good cook, but he did know how to toast a crumpet. Not really knowing what a crumpet was, he explained that it was very similar to the English muffin. I said, "Ah yes. I do think I might have heard of them," and then told Sean that I'd love it for sure if they were anything like English muffins. I have to admit it I liked it a lot.

Without giving any thought to asking me some questions, Liam asked me how old I was. I wasn't even able to give them that much information. I looked up and whispered, "I don't know." Oh God, how I wish I did. That would at the very least be something. Sean jumped right in and said, "Well, anyone can see that you're not a day over twenty-seven!" That brought the first smile to my face since my somewhat spooky arrival the night before.

Every now and then, I'd get a miniscule glimpse of a person or some insignificant element, but regardless of how little or insignificant they were, I still paid very close attention and made very careful mental notes. Those images popped in for only fractions of seconds, but I didn't want to miss anything. At this point, I didn't know what might or might not possibly be of importance. Perhaps my memory of just the small things would surface first. I could tell that this was going to be a long and ongoing process.

Getting serious once again, I told Sean and Liam that I would immediately share anything that I remembered, but I knew that wasn't going to be within the next few hours. I tried so hard not to cry, but I remember a tear running down my cheek. Sean reached over and gave my arm a reassuring pat and told me that he wasn't planning to throw me out into the street. He generously offered to let me stay there as long as needed. That was exactly what I wanted and needed to hear, but I honestly didn't think I would. This man keeps amazing me with his kindness and understanding. From what I know in my heart, they were rare qualities, and I hoped that he knew just how much I appreciated him and Liam too of course. They were both unusual men to put it simply. It was reassuring to know that I wasn't dumped in some serial killer's apartment!

Hearing that was a huge relief to me, but I felt that I should take some responsibility for my own well-being. The weight I felt on my shoulders was insurmountable. I can't rest until I can contribute to the household along with my room and board. As of right now, I can't even buy my own personal needs, like a simple toothbrush and toothpaste! I certainly didn't expect Sean to pay my way. Not knowing how in the world I was going to provide for myself weighed heavily on my heart, but finding out who I was and where I came from were foremost in my mind. And surely someone somewhere would be looking for me. As long as I'm here in Ireland, that means I'm not home, wherever that is. I remember having a career, so I felt sure that a colleague would notice that I'm missing. Then reality really set in. Even if someone did miss me and try to find me, I'd never know it was me that they were looking for as long as my home and name escaped me. Even if my picture appeared in a newspaper or on social media, it would be a one in a million chance that I would see it while I'm here in Ireland. Now my anxiety level is even higher than it was before. This whole mess just seems hopeless.

Chapter 7

The List

By now, Sean has had time to think about and analyze the situation resulting in his perfect plan. Well, almost perfect. He is now boldly taking a stand and quite decidedly announces that we have to put first things first and keep things in their proper perspective. I agreed and said that it was at least a starting point. I didn't expect to hear what he said next!

He stood up and said, "First off, you'll be needing a few things, necessary things," and he politely ordered me to sit down and make a list. He quickly pointed out that the only possessions I had were pajamas, an afghan, a book, and a glass for my wine. As sad as that sounded, he brought the second smile to my face, and again I had to agree. When I smiled, he actually looked as though he felt proud of himself for helping me to feel a little more calm and a little more at ease with my new circumstances.

Knowing that I was in no position to pay for any of this, I did my best to keep the list to a minimum and noted only the absolute necessities. After my list was completed, Sean asked me what my clothing size was. I told him that I wasn't really sure because it depended on what the item was and where it was purchased. In his frustration, he laughed and said, "Good God, woman, just make your best ballpark guess." I told him that I thought most of my clothes were probably somewhere between a six and an eight. With a crooked smirk, he said, "Well, that's at least something I can work with." Then he said, "How about a shoe size?" I did know that much, so I told him that a six and a half would do nicely. Sean ordered Liam to stay with me and not let me out of his sight. He said that he would be back as soon as possible and we were to just sit tight. He threw a deck of cards onto the dining room table and told us to keep busy, so we don't get bored. I wanted to tell him that there was no chance of that happening, but I didn't. I had too much to think about. With that, Sean stepped out the door but instantaneously peaked back through the slightly opened door to tell me that he would offer to take me along to let me pick out what I needed, but he didn't think that I wanted to go shopping in my pajamas and bare feet and that I probably wouldn't feel much like shopping anyway. He said, "Am I right?" I told him that he couldn't have been more right. Sean's short little quick trip turned into two and a half hours. I was beginning to worry and asked Liam if we should send the hounds out to look for him. Liam laughed and said that Sean actually liked to shop and my worrying was totally unnecessary. Just about ten minutes later, the knob on the front door turned, and in walks Sean with both arms filled with bags, and it looked like each bag was filled to capacity. I was speechless, but Liam wasn't. He said, "See, I told you so!"

Sean placed all of the bags on the dining room table and said, "Hey, Princess, come take a look and tell me what you think." When he called me Princess, I was so caught off guard I just looked at him. He just rambled on about not knowing my name and that they would have to call me something, so why not Princess? I told him I liked it, but that I was certain that it wasn't my real name, and I was absolutely certain that I was no princess.

It took me about a half hour to look through everything, but I do have to say he did one hell of a job. For being a bachelor, he must have paid attention to someone at some point because he knew what a lady likes. There's no doubt about it. He didn't miss a thing. He got everything from a toothbrush to deodorant to shampoo and conditioner, and I even found some lovely bodywash and spray. He even thought of a hair dryer and a curling iron, just in case. He also bought new pajamas, a robe and slippers, comfy sweats with matching sweatshirt, leggings, and new slacks with blouses and T-shirts. He even happened to slip in a few unmentionables. I have to say, he has a pretty good eye for size. Most of this stuff wasn't on my list at all! For a moment, it sort of felt like Christmas, but then I found myself thinking realistically. I knew I needed to keep every single receipt because I would be paying him back at some point. I searched through every single bag and article of clothing and couldn't find a single receipt. He was so sneaky and had to have anticipated that I would be looking for them. His kindness and generosity to me is beyond my comprehension. For now, I'll just continue to be grateful and appreciative. I will repay him somehow, some way, some day.

I can hardly begin to describe how wonderful that shower and clean clothes felt. Well, most of the shower anyway. When the spray of the water hit my back, I was quickly reminded that I had lots of healing to do. The force of the water felt as though I had lacerations right down to the bone and the burning sensation was almost unbearable.

With the chaos of the day, talking, crying, getting to know each other, and Sean's shopping spree, we hadn't given a thought to eating at all. It occurred to me that they must be starving. I know I was feeling as though I needed to eat. I decided that I could start showing my gratitude to Sean by fixing dinner for us. I'm no gourmet cook by any means, but I quietly disappeared into the kitchen and started scouting around to see exactly what was available. I'm pretty good at making something out of nothing. Oh my god! While I'm good at making something out of nothing, I wasn't talking about it literally! He had crackers, cereal, crumpets, butter and jam, powdered hot cocoa, a bag of marshmallows, tea, and coffee. With those ingredients, nothing magical was going to appear on the table for dinner. His refrigerator was pretty empty, and there was something in the freezer that was unidentifiable because of freezer burn and ice buildup. Liam walked into the kitchen to see what I was doing. I announced my plan to fix dinner for us, but my grand intentions didn't seem to be working out very well. He said he wasn't surprised because Sean usually got carryout. "I can see that!" I said. Liam shouted to Sean to come into the kitchen to see what I had been up to. After I told him of my plan and what Liam had said about him, he wore that sheepish grin again, he looked down at the floor.

He said, "Yah, I kinda do get carryout a lot." He said that we'd all have to settle for carryout for now, but he would take care of the grocery issue tomorrow. I looked at him and asked if I would be the one making out another list, and we actually had a laugh. It felt so good to laugh.

Because Sean saw to it that I had some of the basics that I needed, Liam generously offered to provide our dinner, and Sean agreed to accept his contribution. After enjoying a really nice dinner of smoked salmon, veggies, and soda bread, we were all feeling rather relaxed and satisfied. We cleaned up and retired to the living room for an after-dinner cocktail. I did enjoy the atmosphere a little more as I drank an Irish cream drink, American style. My mind was again wandering to my impossible situation. The guys both delighted in their usual Guinness beer but realized that I was lost in thought again.

It was obvious that we were all trying to make some kind of sense out of the craziness that we experienced only hours earlier, but we all came up empty. Sean said that we would just have to take it one day at a time and that we would have to be patient. He always seemed to be the sensible, levelheaded one. He felt sure that we would have answers of some sort eventually, but for now, we're at a standstill and just need to wait for those answers.

After having another full day of stress, Liam announced that he was tired and going home. Sean asked him if he would be stopping by the following day. Giving some thought to the question, he said that he doubted that he would because of work needing his attention. He did stress though that if he was needed for anything at all, we were to call him at any time. I thanked Liam for being so gracious and understanding. He walked over to me and gave me the biggest hug of reassurance and said that he thought I was holding up remarkably well, and with a little wink, he said that he thought I was worth it. Even though the hug was painful for me, I welcomed it.

I was feeling a little tired myself, but it wasn't the kind of tired that brings on sleep. I excused myself and told Sean that I'd be back shortly. Now, having my comfy PJs on with my toasty warm robe and slippers, I returned to the living room. Sean offered me another Irish cream. I thanked him but said, "No, one was enough. It's really good but very sweet." I told him that I would have a glass of wine though if that was all right. He jumped up and fulfilled my request before I could blink.

When he delivered the glass of wine to me, he said, "Here you go, ma lady. Wine for the princess." He was bending over backward, trying to make things appear normal. He made lighthearted remarks, trying to make me more comfortable and my circumstances less complicated than they were, but I could also tell that he was trying very hard to hide his own concerns.

Sean had quite a nice library with so many books that I was unfamiliar with, so being the avid reader that I am, I asked if I could browse through his selection. I could see that he was pleased that I took an interest in them and said that he himself loved to read and learn new things. I almost didn't know where to start. Going shelf by shelf, book by book, there it was—the book that I had with me when I popped in out of nowhere was sitting there. I decided that would be a good place to start as I hadn't had an opportunity to finish the last chapter. It turns out that I was right. It really was the best romance novel to hit the market in years. I'm hoping there will be a book number two to follow.

Finishing the last chapter took all of ten minutes, but I was glad that I finished it. It was awesome, and I don't like leaving things unfinished. "Wow! I don't like leaving things unfinished!" I just discovered one more thing about myself that I actually remembered. Sean was right. In time, we just might unravel this perplexing mystery.

Chapter 8

Not in a Million Years

As 11:00 p.m. rolled around, I excused myself and told Sean that I was going to go to bed. I think he could see that I was feeling some apprehension at facing another long night. I never seem to know any more what condition I'll be in when morning comes. The thought of finding myself battered and bruised and not knowing who did it and why was frightening. Many sleepless nights were ahead of me, and I hated it. He walked me down the hall to the guest bedroom, gave me a pat on my arm, and said that he thought tonight would be a better night. Pointing to his room, he said, "That's where I'll be if you need me for anything." In an effort to keep him close by, I asked Sean if maybe he should call it a night too. I think he could see how tensed up I was. He agreed and said he would be in his room after checking to see that everything was buttoned up and the lights turned off.

I can't say that there was no restlessness. I woke up several times during the night. Every time I found myself awake, I panicked and found myself examining my body to see if I had any new signs of further abuse. If I didn't find anything out of the ordinary, I eventually went back to sleep. Somehow I did manage to get some restful sleep for a change though. I felt fairly refreshed in the morning but knew that it would take more than half of a broken night's sleep to renew my strength and energy and I suppose my spirit too. The very first night here, the extraordinary circumstances of the whole experience left me feeling shattered and broken, but I was determined not to feel that way for long. Nothing positive would be accomplished if I allowed myself the luxury of feeling sorry for myself. I'm not that kind of person anyway. I'm a fighter. Knowing that I didn't appear to have unexplained new damage to my body gave me a little peace, at least for that moment.

Over the next several days, all was peaceful and quiet. There were no new events affecting my life. What a blessing that was! From what I could tell, even Sean and Liam seemed to be living their usual routine. Everything was as normal as normal could be; however, in my presence, there was a constant reminder that our lives were anything but normal. Sean and Liam had neglected their work at times because of their concern for me, so it was only natural that I felt some guilt. I assured them both that I was fine and that they should get on with their lives as if I weren't there, but that didn't go over very well. I didn't want to be a burden, but my presence was impossible to ignore. I tried my best to stay out of the way and found myself reading even more than usual, but I was fine with that. And in my attempt to earn my keep by attending to the duties of housekeeping, cooking, laundry, and day-to-day obligations, I felt good about myself. While Sean's apartment wasn't in disarray like most bachelor apartments are, it did need a woman's touch here and there. The exterior of the building was very much like the newer apartments in the states. The layout of the interior was well planned and functional, but only about 1,100 square feet. For a two-bedroom apartment with an additional tiny room that served as Sean's office, you can just imagine how cramped it could get if allowed and only having one bathroom made it difficult at times, but we made it work. The master bedroom was light and airy due to the sliding glass doors that displayed a small deck waiting on the other side. The light from the sliding doors made the king-sized bed with the zigzag-patterned burgundy quilt look striking. The small dresser, with a squatty drip finish modern ceramic table lamp sitting in the middle, rested against the opposite wall and stood just outside the walk-in closet. The guest bedroom was tiny with only a twin bed that was pushed up against the wall. The prominent blue floral comforter made the room look so inviting, and a very small three drawer dresser sat inside the closet to preserve space. The oak parquet flooring throughout the apartment was incredible. I loved it, and it was so easy to care for. The kitchen, much like the rest of the apartment, was small but did have room for a small card table-sized walnut table with a bench tucked underneath and two matching chairs. Sean didn't have a lot of furniture, but what he did have was evidence of his good taste. The unadorned dining table and chairs filled the open area connected to the living room. The leather sofa rested against a wall and was flattered by the painting that hung behind it. Then of course, the red wing back chair that I claimed as my own sat directly across from the sofa.

I no longer had a successful, rewarding career, but I felt that I was contributing and working off a debt that I knew could never be paid—not in a million years.

Not moving forward with remembering the important parts of my life proved to be distracting and frustrating. I needed to remember those details, but for some unknown reason, I was being kept from them. I had to break through that wall, but I didn't know how. Maybe if I quit trying so hard, it will come easier. Settling in to this new lifestyle hasn't been easy for me, but I'm trying to make the best of it, at least until I can go back home.

Never having been to Ireland before, I was hungry to learn more about this beautiful place. As luck would have it, Sean had a most informative book sitting right there on the shelf. Thumbing through this movie on paper pages, I got lost in a world that I didn't know existed. I could hardly read the words because I was so taken with the almost animated pictures and landscape drawings. I never paid much attention to geography before. I can see that not paying attention to geography was a big mistake as I'm getting a taste of what I've been missing, and this is just one country. I think I would like to visit the Cliffs of Moher. It has the most breathtaking view, and the ocean's vastness comes into full focus. One other attraction that caught my eye was the Emerald Isle. For some reason, it feels like I know about the Emerald Isle. I'm sure that I already read about it and perhaps heard it referenced in a movie at some point in time. Then of course, the most popular thing to do in Ireland is to visit the local pubs. The most popular one was called the Guinness Storehouse. If I'm here long enough, I would be most interested in seeing it all! I do know that Sean will give me the grand tour though as he already mentioned that he would show me some of his favorite places in Ireland.

I prepared a somewhat nice dinner. I say somewhat because I've never been accused of being a great cook. Sean asked for seconds, so I was definitely feeling proud of myself and knew that at least this dinner was a success. Our dinners together were always such a pleasant time. On this particular night, Sean was excited and anxious to tell me about a new client that he had just contracted with. As he spoke, his hands were waving through the air as if they had a language all their own, and he could hardly sit still in his chair. He reminded me of a little kid who had just hit his first home run. In his excitement, he informed me that he had been trying to do business with this particular company for a long time. I was so happy to see him happy and excited about something for a change. Worrying about me and how I was getting along had been taking up far too much of his time. I wanted him to revel in his excitement for as long as possible.

After dinner, I tidied up the kitchen while Sean tied up some loose ends in his office. We both finished at just about the same time. Meeting in the living room for our usual evening cocktail, I could tell that Sean still wanted to center his attention on his newly acquired client. The rest of the evening was filled with business talk, but I didn't mind at all. It was a nice change of pace, and I actually liked hearing about his work and took pleasure in knowing that I was important enough to him that he felt he could share that part of his life.

Chapter 9

Connection

I've been here now for slightly over four months, and I haven't experienced any more unwelcome events. Over time and little by little, I found myself enjoying a calm that I hadn't felt in a while, and yet I had to wonder why I was still here. Someone or something is keeping me here, and I don't know why! I'm adjusting to this new life, but I already had a life, and I long to know something about it. Another night crept in, and when I went to bed, I found myself thinking of a likely name that I might have had. I thought that if I verbally spit out names, one might possibly jump out. Every name that I came up with just didn't seem to fit. Nothing sounded familiar. Then, my thoughts turned to Sean. We seemed to have a spiritual kind of connection from the start. I can't explain it, but it was staring us in the face every day. We had spent so much time together I had to wonder if this strange connection could possibly become more than a friendship at some point in time. Was it possible that a relationship might develop and become more than just a friendship? I let my mind wander a bit with this new idea, and before I knew it, an entire hour had passed. Because of this amazing bond that we seemed to have, I knew in my own heart that I wouldn't fight it if he felt as I did, but I also knew that I would not pursue a relationship on my own. The first move would have to be his. If I haven't worn out my welcome by now, I don't think I will at this point, but a personal relationship is so much more than a simple friendship. Sean never made me feel as though I was an unwanted or uninvited guest, but I still didn't even know my name or where I was from and that was a continuous obstacle always with me. Trying to retrieve those memories was my silent task every single day. The not knowing was killing me, so pursuing the answer has become my mission.

It took me an unusually long time to fall asleep. I decided to sleep in the following morning and didn't get out of bed until about 10:00 a.m. I hadn't done that in a while.

I went to the kitchen to make a fresh pot of coffee. Sean was an early riser, and I knew that if there was coffee left over from the pot that Sean had made, it would have been sitting there a long while and surely wouldn't be to my liking. Apparently, my clattering in the kitchen alerted Sean that I had finally joined the living. He walked into the kitchen and said, "Well, good morning, sleepyhead." I smiled and asked him if he would like to join me for a fresh cup of coffee. It was one of those invitations that couldn't be refused. We both loved our coffee. As we sat there, Sean kept inquisitively staring at me. I was beginning to feel uneasy and asked him if something was wrong. He immediately answered, "No, no, absolutely not. I was just wondering how you could sleep in so late after having gone to bed at a reasonable hour." I wanted to tell him the truth, but I couldn't. I couldn't tell him that most of my thinking time was spent wondering about us! That was definitely off limits. I had to think fast, so I just told him that I had a hard time going to sleep. I just couldn't turn my brain off.

Wouldn't you just know it! He had to ask me what thoughts my brain had that were keeping me from sleeping. I made up a few things, but I didn't tell him that I was thinking about a possible future. I told him that I couldn't help but think about taking up an unexpected residence here. His apartment and life must have been so peaceful for him before I came into the picture. I said, "I was pretty much just dumped in your lap."

Much to my surprise, he snapped back very quickly with "Are you kidding me? You're kidding me, right?"

I said, "No, I'm not kidding," and asked him why he would ever think that I would kid about such a thing.

He said, "Because you've been here now for several months. Have I ever made you feel less than welcome? I've never been happier." He told me that it was more like I was heaven-sent and that I was the best thing to ever happen to him. He went on to say that while Liam and he were best friends, Liam was a poor substitute for the sight of or the companionship of a beautiful woman.

He absolutely took my breath away, and I literally had to catch my breath before I could speak. I sure wasn't expecting to hear those words, and I didn't know how to react. After wondering about us just last night, this was all too coincidental. What the hell is going on here? I just sat there for a minute, and he said, "Say something! Anything is better than nothing. Please say something."

My mind was still blank and racing as I searched for the exact right words, but all I could come up with was "I think I'm going to cry."

He said, "Oh God, no! Don't do that. I can't stand it when you cry. I'm so sorry. I didn't mean to offend you in any way." I looked at him, reached over, and touched his cheek and told him that I wasn't offended at all but that I was deeply touched. As he touched my hand, the hand that was still resting on his cheek, a single tear did escape my eye, but I held it together for his sake. Feeling proud of myself for not totally losing it, I told him that his words made my heart happy and warmed as it never has been before.

This was definitely not the conversation that I anticipated having on this particular morning. At that point, I think we were both surprised by the direction our conversation had taken, and we both needed a little time and space to just breathe and digest what had just happened. This conversation took us to a place that neither of us had expected. I didn't know when, but I knew that we would be talking more about this later on. He had made the first move, just as I knew it should be. I can't help but be a little old-fashioned. I must have been raised that way. I have to admit, I was feeling pretty special. I hadn't been special to anyone in such a long time. I recall not having much room for it in my life before because my work was all consuming. That's why I was never close enough to anyone to even think of any kind of a permanent relationship. At the time, I didn't feel as though I was missing out on anything, but now I see how wrong I was. This is what living is supposed to feel like. Perhaps it was written in the stars somewhere that Sean was supposed to be an important part of my life.

Sean spent the rest of the day in his office, other than running to the kitchen to grab a glass of tea. He did run one unexpected errand though. He said that he would only be gone for fifteen or twenty minutes. Knowing that he couldn't keep himself from shopping, I couldn't imagine what he could accomplish in just fifteen or twenty minutes. Sean is never gone for just fifteen or twenty minutes. Sure enough, fifteen minutes later, he walked through the front door. Holding his hand behind his back, he told me that he needed to go into the kitchen alone. I so badly wanted to take a peek, but I promised to stay out until he told me to join him. About two minutes later, he called out my name, that special name that he had given me. As I entered the kitchen and looked around, there, sitting in the middle of the table I found a bud vase with one single red rose standing tall and conspicuously proud. Sean looked at me and said, "That's just one of many more to come." I don't know how he does it, but he keeps finding ways to leave me speechless. I think that this was his way of continuing our conversation without having to say a word. Before I could say anything, he gave me an awkward quick kiss on the cheek and went back into his office to finish up a couple of things and said that he'd be ready for dinner by 7:00. I just stood there, touching my cheek and admiring the beautiful red rose. This was truly a gesture of affection. At that moment, directing my attention to anything else related to reality was nearly impossible. He keeps doing that to me.

I'm sure he wanted to get as much done as possible because he earlier made mention of formally introducing me to Ireland the following day. I was used to venturing out and taking my walks to familiarize myself with the neighborhood, but this is different. I was actually going to see and experience some of Ireland, and he would get no argument from me. I needed a change of scenery and I knew we would be spending the entire day out and about. After dinner, my thoughts kept wandering back to the rose that was sitting in the middle of the table. Sean was in the other room carefully mapping out most of our touring route for our outing the next day. He knew that I wanted to see so many things, so he sought out my approval. It was a sweet gesture, but I certainly couldn't add anything of value. I knew I would love whatever he had planned. Having a limited knowledge of Ireland and its history, I approved of his choices and told him that his plan was well thought-out and perfect. Being a fairly progressive man, I think that was his way of including me in the decision-making. He then suggested that we have a quick night-cap and go to bed so that we would be ready and well rested for our big day out. Sean wasn't in the habit of issuing orders, but he told me in no uncertain terms to be up and ready to go by no later than 9:00 a.m. Even though eating breakfast was not normal for either of us, he was planning to take me to breakfast to start our day and change up our routine.

Chapter 10

Best Day Ever

Replaying the unexpected events that had taken place during the day, I had a hard time falling asleep. Tomorrow's tour was to be more than just basic local attractions of interest. I knew I would love every minute, but I also knew my exploration of Ireland was just beginning.

Sean was on my mind again. In spite of the bizarre, still unknown circumstances that brought me here, I have managed to stay sane, primarily because of Sean. He is the one keeping a careful, thoughtful head on his shoulders. He is the one responsible for my sanity. I can't ignore Liam though. He has been terrific and the only other person on the planet who is aware of my existence. He checks in periodically just to see how I'm doing and always asks if Sean is taking good care of me. He knows Sean well but always jokingly tells me that if Sean isn't behaving, I can always count on him. We always seem to have a good laugh. I'm sure that had I been transported to a place of loneliness; I would have lost my mind by now. I still do have those moments of torment, trying to figure out why and how I got here. I don't think I'll ever be able to forget the feeling I had when I found myself sitting in a strange chair in a strange place. I can't even begin to describe it. Then, to realize the condition I was in after Sean touched my shoulders, I almost can't think about it, but then I realize that I have to think about it. It's such a huge part of the puzzle that I'm trying to put together.

I thank God every night for bringing me to this safe haven. Well, it's a safe haven for now. None of us can possibly know what the future holds.

I finally fell asleep. The hazy morning sun was peering through the window before I knew it. I was up and ready to go out of the door by nine as instructed though. I was so ready. The one little detail that neither of us gave any thought to was the weather. Entering the month of October now, it was pretty chilly out there. I didn't even have a coat. I had no need of one before because I so rarely went out, and when I did, I didn't seem to need one. Sean told me that getting a coat was going to be first on the to-do list. He was a little upset with himself that he hadn't thought of it before. Why would he? I hadn't even thought of it. It was just one of those things, and in the grand scheme of my story, this was pretty insignificant.

We did find a coat that was perfect for me. Actually, it was quite lovely. Again, I found myself thanking Sean for his generosity and thoughtfulness. While he appreciated my gratitude, he let me know right off that he was going to take care of me no matter what. Up until then, I had always taken care of myself and solved my own problems. I've heard that men are natural problem solvers even when there are no problems to be solved. It must be in the DNA. It was kind of nice to know that I could share everything with Sean now.

I had no idea where Sean was planning to take me for breakfast, but knowing Sean, it was sure to be unique. After driving for about twenty minutes, we arrived at this tiny out-of-the-way little place in Kilfenora, County Clare, called Burren Glamping. Sean said that he had never been there before, but it came highly recommended. He always wanted to try it out but never took the time. He thought that this was the perfect time to see for himself. I think he was surprised to see this very curious sight for sure. As we pulled up, all I could see was a type of train trailer car that said, "Horses," on it. The owners had quite an imagination when they converted this horse truck to a small restaurant. They couldn't seat many people, but it was a cute, cozy little place, and much to my surprise the food was incredible.

Now with his curiosity satisfied, Sean and I agreed that it would be one of those places that we will definitely revisit.

I said, "So what other neat surprises do you have up your sleeve, Mr. Murphy? I can hardly wait." Playing very coy, he just looked at me and smiled. He told me to sit tight and enjoy the ride.

I did exactly that. Though the ride took us quite a distance from the city, it was scenic and beautiful, but I didn't know where we were or how much farther we were going. As the landscape was moving by too quickly for me to fully enjoy it, I was still able to marvel at the herds of peaceful sheep that were grazing on the hillside. I don't remember this being on the map that Sean shared with me last night. Before long, I could see a limestone structure off in the distance. I was in absolute awe as Sean told me some of this ancient structures' history. We were approaching "The Rock of Cashel." Sean said that it's in many pictures of the Emerald Isle. It's a grouping of medieval buildings that includes the High Cross and Romanesque Chapel and said that if his memory served him well, he thought that the Round Tower was of the twelfth century and the Gothic Cathedral was thirteenth century. Sean had timed our visit just right as there was an audiovisual show and exhibition about to begin in the visitor's center. I knew we would learn so much more and find out if his recollection was correct. When we finished our tour, we realized that time wouldn't allow us to squeeze in the rest of our originally mapped-out plan, so those sites would have to wait for another outing.

We left in time to grab a quick bite to eat. Breakfast had long worn off, and we were both hungry. Finishing our meal and knowing that Sean had tomorrow's work to think about, I knew it was time to be headed back home. I was a little sad to see our day end, but my entire day had been filled with so many magical surprises. I'm already anticipating another excursion in this awesome place. We arrived home fairly late, around 8:30 or so. We were both ready to get comfortable, and I wanted a glass of wine before bed. Sean was in his office for about thirty minutes and then joined me. He enjoyed his usual Guinness, and we talked about the sights we had seen throughout the day. He seemed pleased with himself that he had made me so happy. As I stood up to walk to my bedroom, Sean walked over and hugged me, kissed me on the cheek, and told me that the best is yet to come. With our arms wrapped around each other, I told him even though I hadn't been there all that long, my experiences here have far surpassed my expectations of life already.

Chapter 11

Lunch with Liam

Walking to my bedroom, I felt as though I was walking on air. It had been a most wonderful day, and I was exhausted. I knew that even if my brain wanted to reenact the events of the day, it would be a short reenactment. The satisfaction that I felt put me to sleep before I could count to ten.

Sean had a business appointment to keep the following morning, and I hadn't gotten up yet before it was time for him to leave. He was always prompt and didn't like to keep his clients waiting. Not wanting to disturb me, he left a note on the counter by the coffee pot, propped up against a salt shaker that said, "I've gone for my appointment. I should be finished around lunch time, but I'm meeting Liam for lunch. We haven't had any guy time in quite a while, and I think he's missing that. I'll see you after lunch. Have a good day." He signed his name at the bottom of the note with a heart drawn near it as if I wouldn't know who left it there. Because the note was situated in a conspicuous place, I read it while I retrieved my first cup of coffee. Never touching the note, I carried my coffee to the living room, picked a comfortable spot, and read while I drank my coffee. At some point, between the time that I read Sean's note and finishing my second cup of coffee, an event took place that I can't even begin to explain. I was totally unprepared for what was about to happen.

At just around 2:30, Sean walked through the door and into total silence. There was no radio on, no TV on, no noise at all. He called out to me but didn't get a response. He thought that was really odd. Walking through the apartment and calling my name, he still couldn't find me. The note that he had written was still on the kitchen counter where he had placed it, and he knew that by the looks of it, I hadn't touched it. A chill ran down his back, and he knew something was terribly wrong.

Now panic began to set in, and he paced back and forth. He desperately tried to think of where I had gone, but he just couldn't imagine a single place. I didn't really know anybody, at least not well enough to disappear like that. The only thing he could think to do was call Liam. It took Liam about thirty minutes to get to Sean's apartment, and by then, he was totally beside himself and in tears. Now, they were well into the evening hours, and Liam tried to calm him, but it was proving to be quite difficult. Sean had a moment of temporary insanity and told Liam that he wanted to go to the police and file a missing person report. Liam just stood there dumb-founded and said, "Are you crazy, Sean? We can't go to the police. What exactly do you think we would tell them?"

Sean looked at Liam as if he was completely defeated and said, "I know. Now that I think of it, that wouldn't be the smartest thing we can do. Sean started to transmit his thoughts out loud as he spoke softly to himself. What would we tell them? Oh, I know. You see, Inspector, this woman we call Princess just appeared one night out of nowhere, dressed in her pajamas with an afghan wrapped around her and a book in her hands. Oh, she brought her own wine too. She has been staying with me ever since because we don't know her real name or where she is from, but she's missing all the same."

Liam said, "Exactly. The way I see it, we have two choices. We can go out and look for her, or we just wait it out right here. She appeared out of nowhere before. Maybe that's how she will return to us now." At least, Liam was thinking with a little logic.

Sean felt as if time was standing still and the hands on the ornate, round wall clock seemed to be moving backward instead of forward. He couldn't help feeling that this was pure hell and couldn't stand the not knowing part or realizing that there wasn't a single thing he could do.

Sean was unable to think clearly, and Liam wasn't far behind. Sick with worry, neither of them slept. They did manage to drink a couple of beers, but their nerves were still totally frazzled. There would be no peace until I returned.

After an unbearable night for the two friends, the morning sun tried to shine through the blinds. The day was pretty overcast, so the sun stayed partially hidden behind the clouds, which didn't help the mood. Never having slept, Sean and Liam were sitting at the kitchen table discussing my disappearance and sipping coffee. They were feeling fatigued by now and so wrapped up in their discussion that they didn't hear me.

Apparently I was sent back to the apartment, just as before. I found myself huddled down and facing the corner by the bookshelf with my hands covering my face. I was paralyzed from fear and couldn't move, and of course I was crying. I thought my days of crying were over and look at me now. I'm right back where I started.

Sean thought he heard a slight noise coming from the living room. After walking around the entire room, he found me tucked away and trembling in my little corner. He ever so slowly walked over to me. He bent down on one knee and barely touched my arm. He was afraid he would startle me and make things worse. His instincts were correct because his touch absolutely did make me cringe, and I pulled away. I didn't know where I was or who had just touched my arm. All I know is that I didn't want to feel anything at that moment. I had already been touched enough.

Chapter 12

Gone Again

Sean spoke to me in the softest voice he could vocalize and kept telling me over and over that it was him, but it just didn't register. I couldn't tell if he was real or not. I couldn't trust myself to believe him. With Sean getting nowhere, Liam told Sean to let him try to connect with me. Sean was reluctant to give up his space near me because he feared that I would disappear again. Liam had to physically pull him away so that he could move closer to me to at least try to get some kind of positive response from me.

Liam tried the same approach that Sean had taken, but it didn't work out any better for him. I pulled away cowering even further down into my little space. Sean told Liam that he had to try again, and Liam was only too happy to surrender his position back to Sean. I know that they were both uncomfortable and frightened beyond measure. Sean kept telling me his name over and over. He assured me that he wasn't there to hurt me. He was so sensitive to my well-being and only wanted to help me. This went on until I realized that I couldn't tolerate crouching in the corner much longer. By now, my legs were cramping up, and I knew in the back of my mind that I would have to take a chance sooner or later no matter how terrified I was. I was about to find out if Sean was real.

Slowly, I pulled my hands away from my face. My vision was blurred from crying, and I was still wary. Sean just knelt there and didn't move a muscle for fear of undoing what little had been accomplished so far. I moved my hands, and that was something at the very least. Although it seemed like forever to Sean, I finally lifted my head and looked up into his eyes. I can't find the words to describe the expression on his face when he looked at me. Tears rolled down his cheeks, and I can remember him whispering, "Oh my god, what the bloody hell has happened to you? Who did this?" I grabbed the front of his shirt with both hands. My fists were filled with the fabric of his shirt, and I wouldn't let go. I remember telling him to hang on to me, tight. I later learned that I told him not to let me go under any circumstance. That's exactly what he did for the duration of this episode. We stayed in that position for quite a while with my face buried in his chest. Then, gradually, he tried to help me stand so that we could walk over to the sofa. I couldn't! My legs wouldn't work the way they were supposed to. Without giving it a second thought, Sean scooped me up and carried me to a more comfortable place where the two of us would fit because I was still hanging on to his shirt for dear life and refused to let go. Liam brought me a cool rag for my face, but I wasn't ready to expose my battered face. I still wasn't at all sure that I was back in the apartment, so keeping my eyes closed kept me from the reality of accepting what may or may not be true. Distinguishing reality from fantasy was incredibly hard. I wasn't ready to take the chance that my newfound comfort wasn't real. They were both so anxious to console me, but I wouldn't let them. All I could do was hang on to Sean's shirt and bury my face deep into his chest all the while staying in my own little world. I was still afraid to look at my surroundings.

I could hear some of their whispers back and forth. They were discussing how I apparently popped back in just as I had before. And just like before, they didn't know how I got back there or where I had been. They certainly knew that I had not been back to my own apartment, wherever that was! After about an hour or so, Sean noticed that I was beginning to relax. He could feel that my hands weren't gripping his shirt as tightly. He asked Liam to gently loosen my fingers away from the grasp of his shirt. Liam was afraid to touch me thinking that I would wake up and try to fight him off! He finally agreed as I wasn't holding on as tight as I had been, and I was becoming more and more relaxed. Knowing that I was probably out cold from pure exhaustion, Liam helped Sean position me on the sofa so that I was comfortably sleeping with my head resting on Sean's leg. My hair was covering my face, and as Liam gingerly placed my favorite satin pillow under my head, he pushed my hair back away from my face. He was going to blot my face with that cool rag, but after finally getting a look at me, tears filled his eyes and he couldn't conceal his emotions. It must have been then that Liam again snapped a photo. This time, it was my battered face that appeared among his many pictures. He didn't say anything and only glanced at Sean because he couldn't find any words to describe how he was really feeling. He needed to step away and leave the room in order to gain his composure. I slept there for the next few hours. Sean never budged though, not once, not even for food or a bathroom break.

I finally woke up, but I could hardly open my eyes. Actually, my left eye was swollen shut, but my right eye allowed me to see a little bit. Normally, anyone in my condition would have been taken to the hospital, but that was impossible in my case. Making up some story about being mugged by a mysterious assailant would be easy, but then I'd have to give them personal information, which I couldn't do! I knew enough about myself, but I still didn't know my name or where I was from, and it was obvious that I'm not from Ireland. That's not like a typical case of amnesia. Sean must have dozed off because when I pushed myself up, off his lap, he was slightly startled. Both he and Liam just looked at me, too afraid to say anything at all. They especially didn't want to ask me any questions. They were afraid to make any kind of gesture at all because they still didn't know if I was back to reality yet or how I would react.

Collecting my thoughts took a minute or two, possibly more. I knew that I was back in the apartment and back to reality, but I almost felt as though I had been drugged. I was woozy, and the room was spinning. Eventually, I was gradually able to focus my good eye, and I wanted to speak, but I struggled with the words. I don't really know when, but in time, I did begin to speak. I looked at Sean first and then glanced at Liam. I didn't feel that I could talk about my recent encounter because my recollection was the same as before. I had absolutely no memory as to what had happened to me. All I could manage to say was "I think I'm hungry." By now, it was late afternoon, almost twenty-four hours later. Sean and Liam both chuckled and in unison said I could have whatever I wanted! Their Princess could have whatever she wanted. With breathy pauses between my words, I whispered, "I think I'd like some coffee and maybe a crumpet."

Sean said, "Coming right up," and helped me into the kitchen. It felt good to stand, so I didn't immediately sit down. Liam asked me if I needed anything. I told him that I needed food and maybe some Nurofen. Nurofen is considered a rapid relief maximum strength pain reliever. Before I could blink, he set a glass of water and two tablets in front of me. By now, the coffee that had been brewing was almost done. The aroma of the freshly brewed coffee and toasting crumpet smelled heavenly. I asked Sean to use a coffee mug of a lighter weight than the big blue one that I usually used. My hands were so sore and swollen from my fingers being clenched together for such a long time, I was afraid I would drop it. Sean set my coffee and crumpet in front of me, and the guys had coffee with me while I ate. They should have been starving but said that they weren't. They kept staring at me with not only a pitiful look of sympathy but also that of relief that the nightmare was over, at least for now.

I finished my coffee and crumpet in what seemed like record time. We started talking a little. They were still reluctant to ask any questions but told me how worried they were and what a very long day it had been. I apologized for having put them through that, but they wouldn't hear of it and were having none of that kind of talk. How dare I apologize for being a victim! I couldn't help but feel guilt, knowing that I was at the center of so much torment. I told Sean that I remembered the indescribable look on his face when he first looked at me. When I told him that, he tensed up, and his demeanor seemed guarded as if he couldn't bring himself to talk about it. I decided that I had already put these two through enough already, so I turned my attention to a hot shower. I knew that I had to look at my current injuries eventually and there was no time like the present, but I had to give myself time to absorb the thought of added injury. Turning the water on in the shower to get hot first seemed like a much better idea. Now, the moment of truth was here. It's now or never. I was talking to myself a lot, but nothing I said could have prepared me for what I was about to see. I just stood there with my eyes closed for a few seconds, and then when I opened them, I just stood there staring at myself. I wasn't ready to see such ugliness. This is not at all what I envisioned. I tried to imagine who and what could have caused this kind of damage, but nothing I imagined was horrible enough, and I started to feel a little queasy. I know this is a little warped and twisted, but I actually started feeling grateful toward whoever had done this to me. At least, they found enough compassion to give me ample time to heal between beatings. First it was my back and now my face! What's next?

My left eye was still swollen shut and a color of purple and blue that I'd never seen before. There were numerous cuts and scrapes on my cheeks, nose, and forehead. When I undressed to shower, I found more, less significant bruises and scrapes but decided to keep that discovery to myself.

I don't think a shower has ever felt so good. I stood there like a statue for the longest time, lost in the simple delight of the comforting warm water raining down on my body. In time, the hot water started to get cooler and reminded me that I had indulged myself long enough. It was time to end this pleasurable experience.

In my haste to console myself, I had forgotten to take clean clothes with me into the bathroom. I immediately realized that little detail when I got out of the shower. I towel dried my hair first and then wrapped a big towel around my body so I could make my escape to the bedroom across the hall. I opened the door slowly and stuck my head out to check to see if the coast was clear. I quickly tiptoed across the hall to my bedroom and closed the door. I could hardly wait to get into my pajamas and robe. I longed for simple comfort now that I was feeling human again.

Just then, there was a little knock on my door. Sean wanted to know if everything was all right since it was taking me so much longer than usual. I assured him that I was absolutely fine and that I'd be joining them shortly. Under the circumstances, I suppose that it's only natural for Sean to be a bit worried. I think that he was checking in to make sure that I hadn't disappeared again.

As I made my way down the hall, he met up with me and asked if he could hug me for a minute. Up until now, he had avoided most physical contact with me because of my initial response. Now he was feeling more confident that I would be receptive to his touch, and he always seemed to know exactly what I need. I think in this instance though, he needed it as much as I did. Since I only had cuts and bruises with no broken bones to be concerned about, I welcomed his hug for as long as he wanted or needed to hug me. I was a hot mess, and the way I looked, I was happy that he still wanted to touch me.

I'm not sure that I was at all ready to give up feeling the safety of his arms wrapped around me, but he loosened his gentle hold, and we walked down the hall and into the living room. Sean told me to pick a comfy place to sit, and he brought me a glass of wine. I had claimed the winged back chair as mine because that's where the "forces" put me on that first night, but tonight, I just wanted to stay near Sean. I wasn't exactly back to being my normal self. Both Liam and Sean could tell that I still needed some space and reassurance that I was in good place, in good hands, and that nothing else was going to happen to me, at least not while they were there in the room with me. They could see that I was still looking warily around the room and not feeling totally comfortable yet. I tried so hard not to let it show, but fooling them was impossible. Sean sat next to me on the sofa, and Liam sat across from us in my wing back chair. Sean could tell that Liam was about to touch on the subject of my disappearance. Knowing that the matter shouldn't be approached just yet, Sean was disturbed by that thought. He quickly changed the subject and asked him how work was going. Liam caught on immediately and interjected some small talk about his job.

I finished my wine but still felt anxious and unsettled. I felt as if I could crawl right out of my skin. My hands were shaky too, but I thought that I was doing a good job at hiding it. When I stood up to refill my glass, Sean cautiously gave me that questioning "really?"

look but then thought better of it and decided that I should have the whole bottle if it made me feel better. He knew that I usually didn't have more than one glass of wine, and to be truthful, I didn't really want another glass. I was making a conscious attempt to avoid being in my room by myself, and one more glass of wine would allow me more time to just "be," doing nothing, going nowhere, and saying very little. We sat quietly for a while not knowing what exactly we were going to talk about. What could we talk about with the elephant still in the room? I knew we had to talk about something, but I wasn't ready to discuss my ordeal. Just to break the silence, I asked Sean if he had been helping Mrs. MacDonald, our elderly neighbor, with anything. She usually needed help with lifting heavy items or just carrying in her many bags of groceries. I swear that half of her load was always nothing but cat food! Now thinking about Mrs. MacDonald, I knew that I would have to make myself scarce for a while. How would I ever explain my appearance to her? I've always been able to hide my abuse beneath my clothing, but this is different. How do I hide my whole face?

Liam finished his beer and said good night. This poor man was emotionally worn out, just as Sean was. I finished my wine and just sat there. After about twenty minutes, Sean could see that I was drained and needed rest. He looked as though a hot shower would do him some good too, but knowing I was restless, he refused to leave me alone. He asked if I was tired and wanted to go to bed or if I was tired but didn't want to be alone. He could see right through me as if he has known me forever. For the entire evening, I thought I had given a pretty good performance, but I didn't fool him one little bit. He reached over me, grabbed the satin pillow that I had used earlier, and put it on his lap. I do believe that he is the sweetest, most caring man I've ever known. Still concerned for my well-being, he ordered me to rest my head on the pillow and sleep. Neither of us would be spending the night alone. He stroked my forehead backward into my hair to put me into a relaxed state. It must have worked well because I fell into sleep very quickly. I can't say that I felt good about his sitting up for the remainder of the night but he insisted.

Chapter 13

The Plan

Morning came right on schedule just as it always had, and Sean was anxious to please me and keep me comfortable. It was totally unnecessary, but he genuinely wanted to wait on me. I was perfectly capable of making the morning coffee, but he insisted that I stay curled up on the sofa a while longer. A short time later, he presented me with my coffee and even remembered to use a lighter-weight mug. I was impressed that he had made note of that.

While we sat sipping our coffee, I mentioned that I knew we needed to talk about my ordeal, but I had no notion of what I was going to say since I didn't know who did this or why. We weren't any closer to figuring this out than we were weeks or even months ago. Not wanting to interrupt the moment we were sharing, I let him know that I would be ready for conversation after I got dressed and ready for the day. He said that whenever I was ready was fine with him. He wasn't going to push me into something that I wasn't ready for.

Although I hadn't been missing all that long, I knew that Sean must have neglected his work during my absence. Knowing him like I do, I knew that he paced the floor with worry the entire time, as did Liam. They truly were best friends.

He said that he did need about an hour to tie up some loose ends. I insisted that he take as much time as needed and tend to his neglected work first. I was glad to have time to think about what the hell I was going to say. Nothing I could think of seemed adequate. Unknowingly to me at that time, Sean had already given great thought and consideration toward moving on to the next step.

In an effort to avoid the inevitable, I suggested that we grab a bite of lunch before diving directly into the deep end. He knew exactly what I was doing and gave me that look, but he did say that we would talk about it when I was ready. I slowly put our lunch items away and straightened up the kitchen. I do dislike a messy kitchen. That didn't take nearly long enough, but I couldn't procrastinate any longer. It was time to move out of my comfort zone and face the problem. I just wish I knew how to approach the unknown.

I met Sean in the living room and took my spot in the wing back chair. Sean sat silently across from me but did not initiate the conversation. He got that look again and said, "You really are going to make me start this conversation, aren't you?" I couldn't deny it. I was still struggling to find something of significance to say. I just sat there, moving my head up and down in a confirming motion.

Sean already knew that I couldn't tell much of a story due to my lack of memory. So he started by telling me that he had consistently given thought to our dilemma over the past few months. He said that he did have one idea but started fidgeting and seemed uncomfortable telling me about it. I tried to assure him that whatever it was, I wouldn't think it was crazy or dumb. I certainly didn't have a plan of my own! In his hesitation, he said, "Okay, here goes!" By now, I was all ears because I hadn't come up with a darn thing. This just might turn out to be a shorter conversation that I originally thought. I trusted Sean and knew that he wouldn't suggest anything unreasonable.

Sean started, "It seems to me that the memory part should be the first thing that we concentrate on." I said that I couldn't agree more and wanted to hear the plan for that. He went on to say that he and Liam had discussed it and decided that we just might want to consider hypnosis. For some unknown reason to me, I know for sure that I've heard of people being hypnotized in order to reveal whatever information is hidden in their subconscious mind. Why would I be so aware of such an action? It must have been a part of my past, but for what part of my past? Sean said, "We need to find someone credible of course. Maybe under hypnosis, you will be able to answer some of our unanswered questions."

While I didn't think that this idea was all that far-fetched, I did need time to think it over. I wasn't at all sure that I wanted someone probing my subconscious mind. What if I had some deep, dark secret that I was ashamed of and didn't want to share? What if something was brought to light that would push Sean away? I told Sean that I needed a couple of days to consider the idea. He understood completely and told me that I should absolutely take the time to deeply think about it. In that time, it's possible that I might even come up with a plan of my own. Since I hadn't up to that point it wasn't very likely that I would now, but it would buy me some time.

Three days had passed, and I could tell that my indecision was gnawing at Sean. I apologized for taking so long but explained that this isn't something that I take lightly and not a decision that is easily made. Since I hadn't come up with a better solution, I told him that I was open to his idea. Even though I am afraid of revealing what I really don't wish to share, just undergoing hypnosis was frightening to me. After giving much thought and energy into making this decision, I decided that I might want Sean and Liam to both be there with me. I wasn't sure at all and was wrestling with the thought of being alone or having them there. They are the only people who truly know my story. It's possible that they might be able to shed some light on some gray area if needed. Ultimately, my mental masturbation resulted in my decision to include them every step of the way. In reality, they more than deserved to hear whatever is revealed, and keeping them in the dark wasn't an option for me. Sean contacted Liam, and together they made it their mission to find precisely the right person for the job. This undertaking was much more difficult than they had imagined and, to date, resulted in nothing but dead ends. As each day passed, their frustration grew more evident. Since so much was at stake, I felt an urgency to find someone, so I did a little investigating on my own too, but I wasn't any more successful than they were. Two weeks later, suddenly, out of nowhere, Liam showed up unexpectedly and could hardly contain his excitement. He proceeded to tell us that he had watched a TV program featuring one particular hypnotist that dealt with issues such as mine. It seems that she has explored many different avenues of hypnosis in her practice. Her name was Dr. Jill O'Hara, and fortunately her office was in a nearby location. Because of her standing in the community and word of mouth, she didn't find that extensive advertising was necessary. That's why they weren't aware of her practice. She already had a full schedule but was always willing to take on new clients in desperate need of her help. I don't think that any one is more desperate than I am.

Sean immediately made an appointment for me. Although our appointment was two weeks out, we were anxious to sit with her for an initial consultation. She needed some background information in order to prepare just the right questions and gather important details. All of this was assuming that she would be able to hypnotize me at all. Some people are resistant to being hypnotized, and I could only hope that I wasn't one of them.

Chapter 14

Patience

It felt as though we were living in slow motion, but I knew that we were finally moving in the right direction. In our anticipation of meeting with Dr. O'Hara, above all else, I told Sean and Liam to make absolutely certain that they would be available to accompany me for my sessions. The more I thought about it, the more I knew that I didn't want them left out, not to mention that they are my only security. There was no way I would even consider doing this alone. Sean told me not to worry and that Dr. O'Hara also insisted that they accompany me, especially for the initial consultation. He had already given her some basic information over the phone. We really had a good feeling about this new approach, so we put our heads together and prepared a few questions of our own for her that we thought were pertinent.

As the days were really dragging on, only three to be exact, I tried to keep as busy as possible, but I was running out of things to do. I was so anxious all the time. I don't think that I've ever experienced that kind of anxiety, and I didn't much like it. The waiting was agonizing. I'm even finding it difficult to do any serious reading. I thought for sure that reading was going to be my saving grace, but as it turned out, I was wrong. Long walks sprinkled in here and there seemed to help. The change of scenery seemed to divert my attention to nature and an occasional dog or cat running from here to there. Going down a different road for at least a little while was welcomed. They say that patience is a virtue, so I have concluded that I must not be very virtuous.

Still having several days to wait, Sean was desperately trying to think of something new that we could do to fill our time each night when he was finished with work. Some of the time, we went out for a slow leisurely dinner in a dimly lit restaurant or even just a long walk together. He tried to keep me occupied with some of the details of his work, but most of the time, I wasn't even paying attention. On other nights, we took in a movie. Liam liked to bowl and suggested that we try that. I like bowling, but I wasn't too keen on that idea because my hands were still slightly sore from gripping Sean's shirt so tight for such a long time. If I ended up dropping the ball, it would surely be on my foot, and I didn't need any more injuries! Besides, I preferred staying in the shadows as my face was still healing and I didn't want to frequent any places with bright lights, such as a bowling alley.

We just have to be patient. There's that word again, patient! I think that I don't like that word very much. With only a couple more days to wait now, my anxiety seemed to build. Now, I was second guessing myself. Had I made the right decision? I just don't know. What if I am a subject that resists hypnosis? My heart would be broken. Was I expecting too much? Will Dr. O'Hara really be able to help me? What if she can't, then I'll be right back where I started. I had so many questions but no answers. Sean and I settled in and decided to watch a movie on TV. It was supposed to be pretty good, and we were both looking forward to it. We asked Liam to join us, and he accepted our invitation. I sat next to Sean on the sofa instead of in my chair because I'd have a better view of the TV. Then, Liam sat next to me on the other side, so there I sat, sandwiched between the two of them.

About an hour into the movie, Sean said that he felt like having popcorn, and Liam said, "I second the motion." We paused the movie only long enough to make the popcorn and refill our drinks. I'm really not a great fan of popcorn myself, but I was only too happy to do something special for them. They had been so attentive to me all this time. I wanted to continue to show them how much they were valued. The opportunity doesn't present itself very often, so when it does, I'm ready to do whatever is required of me.

Just as I was putting the finishing touches on the popcorn, salt, and butter of course, Sean grabbed a couple of beers and refilled my wine glass. That was perfect timing, as usual. I proudly carried my masterpiece down the hall approaching the living room. Almost reaching my destination, I stopped dead in my tracks, and the bowl of popcorn went flying through the air! With my eyes opened wider than I thought possible, I looked at Sean and then at Liam and asked them if they could see what I was seeing. They were looking at me as if I had two heads again. I pointed to the far corner by the bookcase where I had been crouching when I came back. I asked again, "Don't you see that?"

Sean said, "See what?" I must be losing my mind. That thought ended very quickly though because I knew what I was seeing. It was no illusion. I've seen it twice before, and I know that it's real. Standing upright in the corner was that ominous, vague dark shadow that I had seen before. There was no sound or movement coming from that direction. It just appeared to be watching me. I felt as though I was being closely examined or analyzed.

As chills ran down my spine, I asked Sean again, "Do you see that?"

He said, "I'm sorry, Princess, I don't see anything out of the ordinary." I was acutely aware of the shadows that haunted me, but I was unable to pinpoint the original time and place that I first saw them. It's just another memory that I seem to have lost. I was very much aware of the fact that this shadow was much closer to me, but I still couldn't identify the profile. Up to this point, I hadn't mentioned seeing the shadow figures prior to making my dramatic entrance here. I couldn't imagine how it would even be connected to everything that had happened to me, and besides, I had no absolute proof that it actually was. I still wasn't sure that it was, but now my gut was telling me that it was distinctly a part of my nightmare. Disappearing as quickly as it appeared, the incident was over. Now I was forced to tell Sean and Liam what I saw. They didn't actually see anything, so all they could do was take my word for it. This frightening ordeal always leaves me in a panic, and I was visibly upset. I couldn't hide it, so I didn't even try. It's just another piece of the puzzle to figure out. They were a little upset that I hadn't told them that part of the story early on, but they did understand my reluctance to share it since I didn't have proof of it being connected in any way. Sean said, "Oh my god, it has to be connected. How could it not be?" From his reaction, I had to agree, and I apologized for keeping it to myself. They didn't actually see anything, and because they didn't see anything unusual, the only thing they could do was to support me and believe in me. This frightening ordeal left me in a panic. What if they, whoever they are, were my abductors and planning to abduct me again? What if it were to be that very night?

Realizing that I had redecorated the living room, I started frantically cleaning up the popcorn that was scattered every place imaginable. Sean and Liam helped, but they could see that I was moving at a pace that they couldn't begin to keep up with. Sean grabbed my hands and told me to slow down and breathe and to look at only him. His earlier experiences with me told him that I was about ready to break down. By concentrating only on Sean, my heart rate and breathing began to slow down, and I returned to normal. By the time we finished cleaning up the popcorn, Sean said that it was almost too late to watch the rest of the movie. I assertively said, "Oh, no, it isn't. Tomorrow is Sunday, and none of us have to get up early. You wanted popcorn, and you're going to have popcorn, and we are going to finish watching this movie!" Fifteen or twenty minutes later, we were settled in on the sofa and ready to resume the movie where we had left off. I can't say that I was paying very close attention to the plot though. My mind just wouldn't settle down. Liam announced that he already knew what the ending was like and that he was tired and ready to go home, so he did just that. Sean and I had no idea what the ending was going to be, so we were anxious to see the rest of the movie. With the shadow figure long gone, that's what I was focusing on now.

Sean said, "Oh, wait, I almost forgot. There's one more thing I have to do before we start watching our movie."

I had no idea what he needed to do, so I looked at him with questioning eyes and said, "What?" I couldn't imagine what he had forgotten. Before I knew it, he had my face cupped in his hands and was kissing me. I mean passionately kissing me! Oh, my heart, be still. In all the years that I've lived, I've never been kissed quite like that. The gentleness of his hands and tenderness of his kiss made my heart melt. I think it skipped a few beats too! Since I was so caught off guard, the only thing I could do was kiss him back. A kiss like that could make you forget every problem you've ever had, and it surely did! My painful face didn't seem to matter, at least for that incredible moment. He always knows just the right thing to do and when to do it.

Chapter 15

The Big Day

Sunday morning as we were enjoying a leisurely cup of coffee, Sean received a text from Liam. Liam's text asked the question, "So are we going to work more on that list of questions for the first appointment? The big day is just around the corner you know."

Sean responded, "Sure, Liam, why don't you stop by around 3:00 this afternoon? You can even plan to stay for dinner if you want to." A big thumbs-up appeared followed by a smiley face.

I already had a list in my head, but I didn't want to leave Liam out. He had been such a trooper through all this mess. Even though he was the one responsible for discovering Dr. Jill, I wanted him to feel as though he was included and contributed in some way. I was fairly sure that we all had the same questions anyway.

Mrs. MacDonald, the elderly neighbor that called on Sean occasionally for assistance, was knocking on the door. In her feeble little voice, she asked if Sean would help carry her heavy bags of groceries up the stairs and put them in her kitchen. I nudged Sean and whispered, "She means cat food." It was kind of our own inside joke, so he had a hard time keeping his composure even though he was quietly laughing inside.

It didn't take long for this Good Samaritan to carry the grocery bags up to Mrs. MacDonald's kitchen. Of course, she had just baked cookies on Saturday and insisted that Sean take a plateful back with him. If he gets paid like this every time he helps her, I can see why he's so anxious to help. Her cookies are always remarkable. Since I don't know that many people here, I should probably make more of an effort to get to know Mrs. MacDonald. She's a widow, and I'm sure she gets lonely at times although she does have her cats. I couldn't help but smile at my own funny thought of her with her cats. I'm sure she is a lovely lady though. That effort would have to wait until my face was fully healed with no telltale signs of injury. I was almost there but still had a couple of little bruises. Fortunately, I was able to cover them with my hair if necessary. I didn't even want Dr. Jill to see them.

It's Monday morning, and as Liam put it, this is the big day. We have anticipated this day for the past two weeks. In only a few more hours, we will be taking the first step to bringing some light into this darkness and, hopefully, a conclusion to this nightmare. I asked Sean if Liam was going to meet us there or if we were picking him up. Sean said, "We're picking him up, and he is sitting in the back this time!" I laughed, but I had to agree with him. Liam always used his invisible brakes when he sat in the front seat.

We left the apartment a little earlier than planned since we were picking Liam up, but I didn't mind. I loved being out in the fresh air, and this was a most exciting day, especially if this well-thought-out plan proved to be fruitful.

We arrived at Dr. O'Hara's office location about ten minutes early. Sean and I for that matter never wanted to be late regardless of where we were going. We sat in the outer waiting room until Dr. O'Hara walked in and introduced herself. She smiled and said that all of her clients refer to her as Dr. Jill. She felt that by calling her Dr. Jill, the atmosphere was far more comfortable and relaxed, and I couldn't disagree with that. She asked us to follow her into her office and told us to make ourselves comfortable. The big mahogany desk where she briefly sat seemed to swallow her up, but she definitely looked as though she belonged there. The silhouette of her red hair against the light beige leather chair was striking, and her Irish heritage was apparent. Although she was tiny and petite in stature, she was a "take charge" kind of woman. I could really appreciate that because in a way, I pictured myself as being the same. At least, I think I used to be like that. Those memories aren't nearly as vague as others. I wish I knew what I took charge of though.

She handed me a questionnaire to complete while she had a brief conference with Sean and Liam. She needed more information to add to what she had already been told. She knew the basics of my situation but now wanted a more detailed overview. Obviously, I couldn't provide my name, birth date, or where I was from, but I had no trouble with filling out the rest of the form. I couldn't tell what they were saying, but I trusted them completely. Nobody knows my story any better my two rescuers. When I had finished with the paperwork, she motioned for me to join them. Dr. Jill directed us to sit on the beautiful overstuffed leather sofa resting on the back wall of her office. It was almost too comfortable. I wanted to sit between Sean and Liam, and Dr. Jill sat across from us in her own matching overstuffed leather chair. I felt very much at ease and actually looked forward to my next session. That would be the session where we got down to the business of hypnosis.

Dr. Jill indicated that she was going to do a quick assessment to see if I was susceptible to being hypnotized. As she reviewed my questionnaire, I wondered what she had planned. I was more than ready and willing to cooperate in every way possible.

While we weren't undergoing the actual session at this moment, she wanted to make sure that I was comfortable with everything. She tried her best to describe the basics of hypnosis so that I would understand the exact steps that are involved. She went on to say that I would probably feel as if I'm falling asleep but not to worry. That wasn't the case at all. You will feel calm and physically and mentally relaxed. You will have reduced peripheral awareness and an enhanced capacity to respond to suggestion. You will be in a trancelike mental state in which you will likely experience increased attention, concentration, and suggestibility. Hypnosis can't change your basic underlying personality, and I will not make you do anything against your will. She stressed that my well-being would be considered before anything else.

Dr. Jill asked if I understood what she was describing, and I told her that it sounded simple and straight forward. I said that I doubted that I would have a problem with any of it because I didn't feel threatened in any way nor did I feel as though I would intentionally resist being hypnotized. If that was the test, I thought it was extraordinarily easy.

Based on my written answers and on her interview, the assessment was in fact concluded. Dr. Jill was pleased and looking forward to moving on with the plan. She felt that my being hypnotized would produce a positive outcome.

Chapter 16

The Appointment

Fortunately for me, I didn't have to wait long for my next appointment. Liam had shown Dr. Jill the two photos that he had taken so that she could actually see evidence of the severity of my ordeals. I have a new appreciation for Liam's judgment. He had the foresight to record my physical injuries, and I'm so glad that he did. I'm not sure that anyone, outside of the three of us, would ever believe my story without visual proof. It helped Dr. Jill better understand what she was dealing with, and I think to some degree, it helped to put her own anticipated emotions in check. She was stunned by the devastating images of my battered body. Because of the severity of my encounters, Dr. Jill wanted to schedule my next appointment as soon as possible. She indicated that she had never seen anything to compare to the photos she was shown. She herself couldn't imagine that one human being could do this to another unless that person was far beyond being totally sadistic. She told Sean and Liam that the abusive treatment that I had received could possibly cause long or even lasting effects, not just physically but mentally.

We were waiting anxiously for the next appointment day to arrive. It couldn't come soon enough as far as I was concerned. I was constantly looking over my shoulder in anticipation of my next encounter. It could be tomorrow, a week from now, or even several months from now. I just never know. There were never any warning signs to prepare me. Sean tried so hard to keep everything light-hearted. I suppose, to some extent, his attitude kept me a little more grounded than I would have otherwise been.

With the memories of that incredible first kiss, Sean and I were growing closer, but not just romantically. Given my emotional state at times, I can hardly describe the comfort he brought to me. Yet at the same time, I couldn't help but feel that I was a burden that he didn't ask for and that his life would be so much simpler if I weren't in it. Sean didn't feel that way at all and let me know in no uncertain terms that he meant what he said about my being the best thing that ever happened to him. I hugged him and let him know that he was the best thing to ever happen to me too. Just being in the same room with him gave me a feeling of warmth and safety and deep down, I felt genuinely wanted.

Today is a really big day. My session with Dr. Jill was just an hour away. We left to pick up Liam earlier than necessary as we needed to fill the car with gas or, as they call it, petrol. I don't know if I'll ever get used to calling gasoline by the name of petrol. Arriving at Liam's apartment, we found him standing outside waiting for us. He jumped into the car, clasped his hands together, rubbed them in a satisfactory motion, and said, "Well, Princess, this is it! Are you ready?"

I looked at him with some apprehension and said, "I guess I'm as ready as I'll ever be."

When we arrived at our destination, we went straight to Dr. Jill's office. When I walked in, I suddenly had chills running through my body, and I was feeling anxious. I didn't like feeling that way, but I had a bad case of nerves at the prospect of having such an experience. I never entertained the thought of having my brain probed via hypnosis until now. It was a pretty scary thought.

Dr. Jill was prompt in keeping her appointment time with me and seemed anxious to get started. I think she was as curious as we were to see exactly where this journey was going to take us. Dr. Jill's soft, relaxed demeanor put me more at ease, and I was ready to get this session under way. I was happy to hear that my session would be recorded because I wanted to know every single detail.

She proceeded with the necessary steps to put me into a hypnotic state and quickly determined that the result was successful. Making sure that I was in my trancelike state, she then began her cross-examination and made absolutely sure that everything said was recorded for later review.

DR. JILL. Are you relaxed, Princess?

ME. Yes.

DR. JILL. Do you want to begin?

ME. Yes.

DR. JILL. I want to take you back to your apartment the last night when you were there and realized that the side table by your sofa wasn't yours. Can you tell me where your apartment is located?

ME. No, I have no idea.

DR. JILL. Can you tell me your name?

ME. No, I don't know what my name is.

DR. JILL. What state do you live?

ME. I don't know.

DR. JILL. How did you get to Sean's apartment?

ME. I was put there.

DR. JILL. Who put you there, and how did they put you there?

ME. I don't know who put me there or how they did it.

DR. JILL. Why were you put there?

ME. It's my punishment.

DR. JILL. Punishment for what?

ME. I can't tell you now.

DR. JILL. Why can't you tell me now?

ME. Because they are watching me and it's not safe.

DR. JILL. Why don't you remember your name or where you live?

ME. [*short silence*] It's because they won't let me remember.

DR. JILL. Who are they?

ME.: Them! [*My shaking hand was raised with my finger in a pointing position.*]

DR. JILL. Can you describe them?

ME. They look tall.

DR. JILL. What do they look like?

ME. It's hard to see them.

DR. JILL. I want you to relax and take a deep breath. Now try to see them. Can you see them?

ME. Not very well, the light is too bright. [*I'm beginning to show some agitation.*]

DR. JILL. Do you want to go on?

ME. [*hesitation*] Yes.

DR. JILL. What light is too bright?

ME. It fills the room. It's directly above me.

DR. JILL. Can you see anything at all?

ME. Yes.

DR. JILL. What is it that you see?

ME. People.

DR. JILL. How many people do you see?

ME. Many. I can't count them. There are too many.

DR. JILL. What are these people doing?

ME. Nothing.

DR. JILL. How can they be doing nothing?

ME. The ones that aren't standing over me are just laying still.

DR. JILL. What are they lying on, and why are they so still?

ME. They are on some kind of metal table I think. They can't move because they are mentally restricted and sort of in a trance.

DR. JILL. Now what do you see?

ME. [*I'm showing extreme agitation now.*] Oh no! Make them move away from me. They're too close.

DR. JILL. Can you see them better now that they are standing over you?

ME. Yes.

DR. JILL. What do they look like?

ME. Like men I think, but I can't be certain.

DR. JILL. What are they doing?

ME. Oh, they are so angry with me. [*Now I was crying.*]

DR. JILL. Do you want to stop?

ME. I don't know. I don't feel safe now.

Dr. Jill. You aren't in any danger now. You can relax.

Me. But they really are dangerous! [*My anxiety is increasing now.*]

Dr. Jill. Why are they dangerous?

Me. Because they are so angry at me and when they are angry, they usually hurt me.

Dr. Jill. Are they angry with anyone else there?

Me. No, only me.

Dr. Jill. Why are they angry with only you?

Me. Because now that I'm older, I'm too hard to handle.

Dr. Jill. What do you mean "hard to handle?" Can you be more specific?

Me. I won't cooperate with them anymore, and they aren't used to that.

Dr. Jill. Are you telling me that the last two recent ordeals, as you put it, aren't the only ordeals or contact you've had with them?

Me. Yes, exactly. I've been taken by them many, many times over the years.

Dr. Jill. How are you feeling now?

Me. I'm afraid of them. [*I was beginning to tear up.*] They don't want me to talk any more.

Dr. Jill. You are in a safe place now. They can't hurt you. I want you to relax and take a deep breath. I'm going to count backward from three to one. When I reach one, you will awake feeling refreshed and peaceful. Three, two, one.

Me. When are we going to get started? I'm so ready.

Dr. Jill. We already did, and we've finished this session. You did great, but we will have to continue in your second session. "Second session?" I said.

Dr. Jill said, "I think we will make great strides, but we have to take baby steps to get there. I'm going to set up another appointment so that we can learn more."

I asked, "May I listen to the tape now? I'm so curious" Dr. Jill said that she didn't think that would be wise. I indicated that I had heard her answer but had to ask if she would at least tell me what my name is.

"No, not just yet," Dr. Jill responded. I was so confused and said that I thought that was the whole point of taping the session!

"But why?" I asked. That surely can't be a secret! Dr. Jill said it's not that easy. She told me that she asked me about my name and where I was from, but we still don't know the answer yet.

"Seriously?" I asked. Dr. Jill was quick to add that perhaps we will know more after my second session. She said that she had no intention of keeping the tapes from me, but for now, she didn't want to risk my being influenced by anything that was said here today and that we will pick up where we left off the next time I see her.

Dr. Jill said, "It's imperative that we start each new session cleanly. I know how anxious you are to know everything, but please believe me when I tell you that I do know what I'm doing." I asked her when my next appointment would be, and she checked her schedule. "Thankfully, it looks like I have on opening for the day after tomorrow at 1:00 p.m.," she said.

After having said that, she looked at Sean and Liam and asked them to respect her decision not to share any information right at this moment, and they promised to keep everything that they heard to themselves. Due to my half-hearted thank-you, when we left, she was aware of how disappointed I was in the outcome of this session. I was so hoping that this would be an easy, cut, and dried process and that the answers would come quickly. Boy was I wrong!

Chapter 17

A Kiss, a Hug, and some Wine

On the way home, we decided to stop for a bite to eat. After being seated at our table, I looked at them, batting my baby blues a few times and said, "Now that we aren't in the presence of Dr. Jill, tell me what happened."

Sean just looked at me, widened his eyes, and said, "Really? You're really asking us to go back on our word? You know that we promised not to say anything, and that's that, so don't ask again!" I agreed, but I told them that I didn't think it was fair to keep me in the dark. Sean said, "I totally understand, but believe me, you'll thank us later. You will know everything when the time is right." I wasn't entirely sure about that but for now, all I could do was trust them as I had grown accustomed to doing.

We ate our meal and left to drop Liam at his apartment. I thanked him for his interest in my crazy life and confirmed with him that he would be accompanying us for the next appointment. He took my hand and said, "Princess, after the session that you just had, wild horses couldn't keep me away," and added that he wouldn't miss it for anything! That just added to my anxiety, and now I was more curious than ever to know what had happened.

Sean and I headed back to the apartment and arrived just in time to help Mrs. MacDonald carry in her new ladder. Sean tilted his head and asked her why she thought she needed a five-foot ladder. It was aluminum and lightweight, but still, it was considerably more than just a step ladder. She said, "My other one broke, and I have to clean my ceiling fans." We looked at each other with wide eyes and then back at her. Sean told her that he would be more than happy to help out with that. "I know you would, but I want to do it now, today," she said. She was never shy when it came to conveying her messages. We weren't planning to add any cleaning to our day, but Sean carried her ladder to her apartment and told her that he'd be right over. He knew it wouldn't take all that long to clean a couple of ceiling fans. I was glad that he offered. I didn't want us to be responsible for this cute little old lady breaking a leg or some other part of her body!

As usual, Sean walked through the door holding a plate of that week's freshly baked cookies. I was beginning to understand why Mrs. MacDonald was a little on the portly side. I had to be careful that I didn't follow in her footsteps, but I did enjoy reaping the rewards of her talents.

We changed into our comfy clothes and agreed that it was time to just sit and relax. Sean asked me if I wanted anything, and of course, I did. I told him that I wanted a big hug, a big kiss, and a glass of wine, all in that order. He smiled and said, "Funny, I was just thinking to myself that you needed exactly that!" He was extremely happy to honor my request. While hugging me and with a coy look on his face and of course batting his big beautiful hazel eyes (wonder where he got that idea), he asked, "Is there anything at all that you would like to add to your list?" I knew exactly where he was heading with that question and told him that there was, but I wouldn't add it to the list until later. I wanted to keep him filled with anticipation. I told him that he had already taken care of the big hug part so now all he had to do was fulfill the rest of my request. A big kiss and a glass of wine would do nicely for right now. He smiled, kissed me, and handed me my wine. We were discussing the day and enjoying each other's company when I again looked at him with questioning eyes. In his phenomenal connectivity to me, he was very well aware of what I was doing and said, "Don't even go there! It's not happening! You heard what Dr. Jill said." He told me that I'd just have to be patient. There's that word again! It's so annoying.

Anticipating what the evening might hold for us, I asked for another glass of wine. I was a little bit nervous, but I didn't want to show it. I wondered to myself, "Why do men always seem so sure of themselves in the bedroom?" The answer to that question was, of course, they're not! They get just as nervous as we do. But Sean certainly didn't act like it. Either he hid his experience or inexperience well, or he really wasn't nervous at all.

I do know one thing though. Thinking about our possible later activity definitely took my mind off the session with Dr. Jill today.

I finished my wine and walked to the kitchen to clean the wine glass that I had just used when I heard Sean turn off the TV. Before I could even dry the glass, he was standing in the kitchen with me. He waited for me to finish what I was doing and then walked up behind me, and wrapping his arms around me without missing a beat, he twirled me around and grabbed my hands. He slowly walked backward, pulling me along with him. I knew we were heading to his bedroom, and my heart felt like it was going to pound right out of my chest. I almost couldn't breathe.

He picked me up and laid me on the bed, then looked at me, and slowly leaned toward me until his lips were nearly touching mine. He was definitely experienced, a bit of a tease, and he was no amateur when it came to kissing. The mutual passion that was shared between us was overwhelming, like nothing I've experienced before. He gently climbed into bed and moved as close to me as he could possibly get and passionately kissed me. I was nervous and sure that my inexperience was showing by now, but responding to him was as natural as breathing, and all I needed to do was follow my heart. The rest came easy. The foreplay was intensely indescribable and provocative. As we traced each other's body with our hands, our lips locked again. As he moved on to nibble my ear and neck, I whispered that I wanted him so very much. He moved his body slowly on top of mine and took me straight to heaven. Our connection was strong, and everything felt right.

The feeling of gratification filled the room with silence, but we truly enjoyed the sensation and comfort of still being in each other's arms. It seemed as though we were meant to be together, but that thought seemed strange considering we lived thousands of miles apart and had never heard of each other until a few months ago. We drifted off to sweet sleep.

Chapter 18

Quiet Day

It was about 9:00 when we woke up the next morning. With our arms still tangled together, neither of us wanted to leave the bed or each other for that matter. We stayed there peacefully, enjoying each other's arms until the last possible moment that Sean had to ready himself for another appointment with his new client. Sadly, we didn't have time for more than that, but I knew that we would be sharing many more nights together.

With Sean now gone, I took my turn in the shower. I still didn't have a hugely expansive wardrobe, so deciding what to wear wasn't very difficult. Sean is planning to take me on a shopping spree, but over the past weeks, our minds weren't exactly on shopping, and most of Sean's time has been occupied by much more pressing and important things.

I sat quietly enjoying my morning coffee when a funny thought entered my head. Even though I was sitting there by myself, I started laughing. I was thinking that Sean would surely want to meet with Liam for lunch. I'm sure that Liam suspects that we are more than just roommates by now, and Sean was probably going to want him to know that he got lucky last night! That's just how guys are, most guys anyway. Giving greater thought to it though, I'm not so sure that Sean would share something so beautiful and personal with Liam.

Oh, who am I kidding? Of course, he did. After all, they've been best buds forever.

Not knowing how long Sean's appointment would last or what his plans were, I decided that I should get moving and do something productive before the day totally escaped me. I found plenty to do. Keeping busy and of course thinking about last night kept my mind occupied. It didn't leave much time to think about or wonder what I revealed in my first session with Dr. Jill. It was so hard not knowing the details, but I did have complete faith and trust in the care that I was receiving. Sean and Liam seemed very comfortable with Dr. Jill, so I figured that I should be too. Liam said that he could see why she had the reputation that she had and was totally impressed.

So far, the day had been uneventful, and that was just fine with me. I stripped the bed and put the sheets into the washing machine. To save myself a little time and trouble, I decided to wash, dry, and reuse the same set of sheets. Folding king-sized sheets was exhausting and wasn't my favorite thing to do. Sean came home right around 4:00 and suggested that we go out for an early dinner and, then if we felt like it, maybe take a drive around town. He knew of a couple of little shops that would have the type of clothing that I liked. I really did need to expand my wardrobe, so I was open to his suggestion. Who doesn't like to shop for new clothes?

Sean wanted me to model everything that I had picked out. I'm not sure why because he knew that I would probably get the things that I liked, not necessarily the things that he liked. I was in luck though because we agreed on the very same outfits. I wanted him to be proud of the way I looked, and besides, he was paying for everything so he should have some say in the matter.

I do miss working, but getting a job right now is impossible. I wasn't positive that I had a professional career before, but I felt as though I did. I wish I knew what it was. Any prospective employer would want a name, address, and I'm sure an ID, such as a driver's license, and I couldn't produce any of it, well, maybe except for the address, but I could hardly tell them that my name was Princess! No last name, just Princess! I know that in the United States, we have social security numbers, not that I could remember what mine was, but I had never given any thought to it here in Ireland. Do they even have such a thing? At some point, I'll have to do a little research on that.

Sean liked taking care of me and frequently told me so. I was glad that he had a good job so that I wasn't a total drain on his finances, but I was still uncomfortable with him being the one doing all the giving. He was my emotional, mental, and physical support and of course my financial support.

I think that Liam was as anxious for my next session as I was. He sent a text to Sean to confirm my appointment time for the following day. He wanted to be sure he was ready and waiting on time. He was kind enough to shuffle his work schedule to accommodate me and my crazy life. That meant it was necessary for him to work some evenings to make up for whatever he didn't accomplish during the day. With Liam also having a home office, it made things much simpler for him too. He insisted that it wasn't a problem and he was more than happy to do it. He told me that before I came along, their lives were pretty boring. He positively couldn't say that they were bored anymore, and I don't think that this kind of excitement was something that either of them had ever wished for or had in mind.

After making it back home, going through my new attire made it seem like it was Christmas for a second time. I looked forward to dressing a little more nicely for my next appointment with Dr. Jill. I wanted to look nice, but I also wanted to be comfortable. I've gotten used to being comfortable over these past few months, and I didn't want to give it up for the sake of fashion.

Sean and I had a very full day, and we were both tired. Just being together and enjoying each other's company was the plan for tonight. An arm around me and a kiss was all I needed. Sean told me that I had to give up the guest room because from now on, his bedroom was my bedroom. The dressers and closet needed a little rearranging, but I was up for the challenge. I decided that I could utilize the closet and dresser in the guest room if necessary. Sharing a closet with Sean could be a potential problem. Sean was a pretty nice dresser himself, so his closet space was limited. His wardrobe wasn't over the top at all, but he had many thoughtfully put together outfits that suited him.

Chapter 19

Session Two

It is another huge day for us. I use the term "us," but I was basically more focused on myself wondering what would be revealed this time around. I wanted today to be the first day of the rest of my life. I wanted today to be the day that I learn exactly who I am and where I came from. I know that after this length of time, it didn't really matter to Sean and Liam, but it meant everything to me. That is my identity. I reassured Sean that if I did find out who I was, nothing between us would change. I planned to stress to Dr. Jill that my ultimate goal, no matter how hard she has to push me, is to know who I am and where I'm from.

My appointment time was nearing. We had just enough time to pick Liam up and make it there a couple of minutes early.

As she had done before, Dr. Jill greeted us with a smile and a positive attitude. It must have been catching because I felt more and more at ease around her every time we met, but my mouth was so dry today. I'm sure it was because of my nerves and my eagerness to start my session. I anticipated this session as being the session that would reveal all. Dr. Jill gave me a bottle of water and told me to make myself comfortable between Liam and Sean, just the same as before. Dr. Jill asked if I was ready to begin. I replied that I was ready yesterday and the day before. "I'm sure you were," said Dr. Jill. "All right then, let's begin."

Apparently, I am easily transitioned into a hypnotic state as I was in the expected trance very quickly. Dr. Jill was ready to begin.

Dr. Jill. Are you relaxed, Princess?

Me. Yes.

Dr. Jill. Are you ready to continue?

Me. Yes.

Dr. Jill. Today, I'd like to take you back to the time that Sean found you crouched in the corner, when you were covering your face. When you were gone from the apartment that day, where did you go?

Me. To the same place as before.

Dr. Jill. Where exactly was that?

Me. I don't know. There aren't any windows. It looks like a regular kind of room with computers and all.

Dr. Jill. How did you get there?

Me. They took me there.

Dr. Jill. Who are they?

Me. They are monsters and very mean to me.

Dr. Jill. Why do you call them monsters?

Me. Because they are brutal and ugly, and they don't seem to have feelings.

Dr. Jill. Why are they mean to you?

Me. Because they know I'm different than the others.

Dr. Jill. How are you different from the others?

Me. I have an echoic and eidetic memory, and they fear that.

Dr. Jill. Is that the only difference between you and the others?

Me. No, the others always do exactly what is expected of them, and I refuse to cooperate with them like I did when I was younger.

Dr. Jill. Why don't you want to cooperate with them?

Me. Because they want to manipulate me and use me.

Dr. Jill. So if you resist their manipulation, what do they do?

Me. They always hurt me, and I become a victim rather than a helper or study subject.

DR. JILL. Wouldn't it be easier for you to just cooperate?

ME. Oh yes, but I refuse to be manipulated into doing something that I know is wrong.

DR. JILL. What are they doing now?

ME. They… [*I'm getting visible upset*] They have attached things to my head. No! Make them stop! It hurts!

DR. JILL. They've finished, and you don't feel any pain. Take a deep breath, Princess. Can you tell me what else they do to you, or would you rather stop?

ME. No, I can continue for a little while I think.

DR. JILL. Could you tell exactly what they were doing to your head?

ME. I'm not sure, but they put some kind of rod or probe into my eye. They… [*Now I'm crying.*] poke and prod and stick things into my body. I try to fight them, but unlike the other subjects, they have me in restraints!

DR. JILL. The restraints are off now. You are in a safe place. Are you relaxing?

ME. Yes, that's much better.

DR. JILL. What part of your body do they like to explore?

ME. Every part that they think is important to study.

DR. JILL. So that's pretty much your whole body?

ME. Yes, but they are especially interested in my brain!

DR. JILL. Why do you think that is?

ME. They can't totally remove all my memories like they do to most, and they hate that.

DR. JILL. Why would they want to take all your memories?

ME. So that I can't expose them. They are afraid that I will remember too much.

DR. JILL. Expose them?

ME. Yes, they don't want anyone to know that they exist.

DR. JILL. Let's move on to a different place now.

ME. Yes, I'd like that.

DR. JILL. Can you tell me your name and where you come from now?

ME. No.

DR. JILL. Why is it that those memories are so hard to recall?

ME. Those memories will never come back. They made sure of that.

Dr. Jill. Why was removing those particular memories so important to them?

Me. They wanted protect themselves, and they wanted to make an example of me, just in case the others didn't want to follow orders.

Dr. Jill. You are lying on the table again. Are you alone?

Me. No, I'm never alone.

Dr. Jill. Why aren't you ever left alone?

Me. Because they don't trust me.

Dr. Jill. What is happening now?

Me. [*I'm crying hysterically now with my knees brought up to my chest.*] Oh no! They don't like what I'm thinking, and they are so very angry. Make them stop hurting me! They're doing something to my eye again, and they're hurting my face.

Dr. Jill. You can relax now. You're safe and comfortable. I want you to take a deep breath. I'm going to count backward from three to one. When I reach one, you will awake feeling refreshed and peaceful. Three, two, one. You can open your eyes now, Princess.

I asked if the session was over, and Dr. Jill said yes. I felt fine and rested, but from the way my eyes felt, I must have been crying. "Was I crying?" I asked.

Sean put his arm around me and told me that I was indeed crying. He said, "I'm with you now. You're safe, and you don't have to worry about anything." As I always did, I felt safe and comfortable in Sean's arms. The connection that we had didn't feel normal. It was so much more than just an attraction for one another. A logical explanation of this eluded me for now, but I was sure I'd eventually figure that out too.

"Well, Dr. Jill, how did it go? Did you learn much more about me?" Dr. Jill said that she learned quite a bit more about me and my character. I asked her what she meant about my character, and she said that I seemed to be a very strong-willed, determined person. She told me that through most of the session, she was focused on gathering information about my whereabouts when I experience my disappearing episodes. She said, "I want you to know that I did ask about your name again and where you come from. Unfortunately, we still don't have an answer." My chin dropped to my chest, and again I was so disheartened. That's that one thing that I am most interested in finding out, and we're getting nowhere.

I was intently listening to everything that she said, but again, I was extremely disappointed to hear that she couldn't share the tapes with me right now. She assured me that I would have a better under-standing when we moved further along, perhaps in the next session, but that she couldn't make any promises. She said, "Your story is going to take longer to unravel than I originally anticipated. There's much work to be done here, and I can't give you a specific time that I will be releasing the tapes. I promise you though, at the end, I will fill you in with summaries of each session and you'll be given the tapes so that you can listen to every word."

Dr. Jill asked me to have a seat in the waiting room. She said that she wanted to have a short word with Sean and Liam. I wasn't too keen on being left out again, but I wasn't about to argue with her. Dr. Jill told Sean and Liam that so far, she has been able to keep things fairly calm with her questioning. The next session might get a little messier and a lot more upsetting. It was way too hard to predict what my reactions to her questions were going to be. They understood and knew that Dr. Jill needed to press on, even if it was unpleasant.

The door opened, and Dr. Jill asked me to join them once again and checked her appointment book to set up my next visit. Because she anticipated having to pursue this further, she kept a time open for two days later. She didn't want to let too much time lapse between appointments. She was extremely concerned for me and expected additional abductions to occur, especially now that I was telling a story that was supposed to remain concealed.

Chapter 20

A New Surprise

After leaving Dr. Jill's office, we followed our usual routine. This time though, Sean and Liam could see that I seemed more uptight and nervous than usual. I was clasping my hands together, rolling my thumbs around and around and scanning the room. I don't know why I thought I needed to scan the room, but it made sense at the time. Perhaps I thought that the dark, shadowy figure was going to show up off in the distance to continue scrutinizing me. Sean reached over and held my hands in an attempt to calm my nervousness, and I just stared at him. Not knowing anything about my sessions with Dr. Jill was killing me. I told him in no uncertain terms that I refused to be kept in the dark any longer and that no matter what, after the next session, Dr. Jill would be sharing at least some information with me! If she didn't, I just wouldn't go back! Sean begged me to please trust them and Dr. Jill. He said that I would totally understand later why Dr. Jill found it necessary to withhold information and that he felt it would do more harm than good to divulge too much right now. Liam agreed with Sean but added that he was surprised that I had just told them off! They weren't used to my being so assertive. This was a whole new side of me that they were seeing for the first time. It definitely is a little out of character for me, so I'm sure they didn't quite know what to do with that.

I was ready to place my order at this point, so Liam motioned to the waitress to come to our table. She couldn't get there fast enough for him. I think my being so aggressive really rattled him. Actually, it felt good to speak up and tell them in no uncertain terms what I was thinking. I was tired of being patient, oh that word again! No more patience for me. It was time to get serious and down to brass tacks. Getting that off my chest felt as though a weight had been lifted, and I was looking forward to my next session. I realized that I was starving and wanted my food. I get cranky when I'm hungry. These poor guys have to put up with all of my shortcomings and little idiosyncrasies. They should get an award of some kind!

Sean and Liam had both planned to take the entire day off so that they could devote their time that afternoon to only me. I don't know why they thought they needed to do that, but I'm so incredibly lucky that I can share everything with them and even luckier that they are best friends who truly care about me.

With their brains searching for new ideas and new things we could possibly do, we ended up just driving around the countryside. I didn't mind that at all. Ireland was still so beautiful and new to me. No matter what direction my eyes took me, all I could see was a sea of emerald green. We hadn't driven all that long when Sean told me to keep looking to my right. Liam seemed to know where we were going, but I surely didn't. We were approaching a strikingly typical, quaint Irish cottage with a long driveway leading up to the front door. Sean turned and slowly made his way up the sandy gravel road to where the cottage stood. I said, "What are we doing here? It looks like private property."

Sean said, "It is private property." I just sat there thinking that he's lost his mind. He wasn't filling in the pieces of the story fast enough for me, but he finally told me that he had grown up there. His mum and dad had moved some time ago. He explained that they now lived few hours driving distance from there, and when they left the cottage, they didn't sell it. Instead, they signed it over to Sean.

I was astonished and said, "And you're just now telling me this? Why didn't you tell me before?"

Sean said, "I can't really answer that. I guess it didn't occur to me that you would be all that interested in seeing it." I called him a big goof and told him that he obviously still had a lot to learn about me.

I turned my eye piercing look in Liam's direction and said, "That goes for you too!"

Sean said that he hadn't considered living there now because he needs an adequate cell and Internet service for his work but went on to say that he thought it might be a good weekend getaway place in the future. I couldn't agree more.

He was reluctant to take me inside, but I insisted. He said that he hadn't been there in a long while and that I shouldn't expect much. He opened the door and motioned for me to go ahead of him. I felt as though I had stepped back in time. It was absolutely adorable and had so much potential. I asked Sean if he would consider fixing it up so that we could use it for those weekend getaways. To my surprise, he immediately said yes but that he wouldn't consider it until my sessions with Dr. Jill were completed. Knowing that he felt strongly about this, I didn't want to make a big deal of it, but I was of a different opinion. I felt that it would be something new to look forward to and it would be a great diversion from the seriousness of my sessions. I was secretly hoping that maybe I would be able to change his mind at some point.

I was so preoccupied with something new to focus on; all I could think about was fixing up the cottage. I had so many great ideas. This little cottage became the best distraction ever, and I so welcomed it even though I was only cultivating new ideas in my head for the renovation and not physically doing anything for the time being.

Chapter 21

Session Three

My third session with Dr. Jill was only hours away now, and I was trying to decide if I should rehearse my speech about insisting on hearing what these sessions were revealing or if I should listen to Sean's advice.

Sitting in Dr. Jill's waiting room a little longer than usual, I was beginning to get anxious and tense. I wasn't paying attention to anything around me, and Sean could see that I was growing more and more concerned. In an effort to direct my mind to something else, he asked me how I wanted to decorate the cottage. Oh, he's really good! Now my brain was fixed on picking out fabric for new curtains while we waited. There he goes again! He's always good with distractions and seems to know exactly how to calm my anxiety.

Dr. Jill appeared in the waiting room and said that she was ready for us to join her. We walked in and took our usual positions on that beautiful, overstuffed leather sofa. Dr. Jill asked if I was ready to begin, and I told her that I was, but before we get started, I wanted to express my thoughts to her. I had decided to voice my opinion. Dr. Jill said, "What's on your mind?" I repeated the words that I had previously spoken to Sean and Liam about this being my last session if she was still unwilling to share some of the tapes with me. Because I was so strong-willed, she said that she had already anticipated that and was prepared to accommodate my needs, at least a little. I expressed my approval and told her I was ready to begin. Still transitioning easily into a hypnotic state, I fell into a deep trance very quickly. Dr. Jill was ready to begin.

DR. JILL. Are you relaxed and ready to begin?

ME. Yes.

DR. JILL. I'd like to pick up where we left off before. Is that all right with you?

ME. Yes.

DR. JILL. You are now back to the place where they didn't like what you were thinking, but this time, it will be more like you are watching a movie and you won't feel as threatened as you were feeling before. Do you think you can do that?

ME. I'll try.

DR. JILL. What were you thinking that made them so angry?

ME. I was thinking that they kept changing.

DR. JILL. How were they changing?

ME. I thought that they were changing their appearance to keep me confused.

DR. JILL. Do you think they had the ability to do that, or was it just an idea that you had?

ME. I really can't say, but something made me think it.

DR. JILL. Why do you think that just a thought made them angry?

ME. Because they felt I was getting too close.

DR. JILL. Too close to what?

ME. Too close to seeing their real identities.

DR. JILL. With their reaction of anger, did you feel as though you were possibly onto something?

ME. Because they became more infuriated with me, I would have to answer yes.

DR. JILL. What did you think their real identities were?

ME. I still don't know for sure. At times, I thought they were men, but every now and then, they didn't look like men to me.

DR. JILL. What did they look like?

ME. You won't believe me if I tell you.

DR. JILL. Oh, but I will. Please tell me.

ME. I don't know if I can now.

DR. JILL. Why is that?

ME. They're watching me again.

DR. JILL. When you are back to being comfortable, you can tell me then. Is that acceptable to you?

ME. Yes.

DR. JILL. I will wait, and when you're ready, you just tell me.

ME. [*Two or three minutes had passed.*] I think it's safe to talk now. Occasionally they look like they aren't human. They have two arms and two legs but have a different appearance.

DR. JILL. In what way do they look different?

ME. Their skin seemed very rough, and they were a dark color, and they didn't seem to have any humanlike features.

DR. JILL. Do they change appearance often?

ME. Only when it suits their needs, but I'm still not sure if they are actually changing their appearance or if they are just entirely different people altogether.

DR. JILL. When it suits their needs? What do you mean?

ME. I mean that they do whatever they want, whenever they want.

DR. JILL. What is it that they are doing that's so important to them?

ME. I think they want to study us. They want to know how we are made, inside and out. Of all the others that they have encountered, they find us the most intriguing. However, even though our intellect is incredible, they view our intelligence as being inferior to theirs most of the time. I'm pretty sure that I have upset that theory. They never thought that they would encounter someone like me.

DR. JILL. Is a certain level of intelligence the same for all their study subjects?

ME. Absolutely not! How do I put this without being offensive? Excuse this description, but some are absolute morons and others, like me, are exceptionally intelligent.

DR. JILL. Others like you? What do you mean?

ME. I can't tell you now. They're watching me again.

DR. JILL. Let's move on to something else then. When they hurt you, can the others see what they are doing to you?

ME. Yes, at times. As I said before, they want to make me an example of what will happen to them if they don't cooperate.

DR. JILL. Do they always keep everything they do out in the open?

ME. No, they have private rooms too.

DR. JILL. What do they use the private rooms for?

ME. Horrible, unspeakable things. [*I'm extremely agitated now, and I just want to run.*]

DR. JILL. You're in a safe place. You can relax and take a deep breath. They can't hurt you. Are you comfortable telling me more, or do you want to stop?

ME. I can only tell you that they haven't finished with me yet! I never want to go back, but I know they can take me whenever they want. The thought of going back there is almost unbearable.

DR. JILL. I think we've covered enough for this session. I want you to take yourself to a safe place and relax. I'm going to count backward from three to one. When I reach one, you will awaken feeling totally refreshed and relaxed. Three, two, one, you can open your eyes now.

Dr. Jill knew that she would have to share some of the information with me or I wouldn't return for a fourth session. She very carefully chose only those parts she felt safe in sharing, which was next to nothing. She would share only the parts that she thought wouldn't upset me too much and only the parts that wouldn't reveal too much. She didn't actually allow me to hear any of the tapes, but she did give me little bits and pieces of my sessions.

Her disclosure didn't exactly satisfy my appetite for information, but I couldn't make her divulge information that she thought would be harmful at this point. I suppose that I had heard just enough to appease my curiosity. She explained to me that the deeper we traveled into my subconscious mind, my emotional well-being would remain to be her primary concern and that my mental and emotional state would be the determining factor in deciding when or even if we continue or not. Risking any kind of harm to me was absolutely not an option. I agreed but wanted to go on. There was obviously so much more to learn. I needed to know more, and as observers, she, Sean and Liam wanted to know more just as much as I did. Each new session revealed so much more than the one before. Once again, Dr. Jill asked me to take a seat in the outer waiting room so she could have a word with Sean and Liam. It was so upsetting, and I didn't like being left out. What are they discussing that I shouldn't hear?

Being even more serious than the last time, she told Sean and Liam to be very careful about not discussing any information that she hadn't already shared with me. She didn't feel that I was ready to hear more nor was I in a very stable mental place. She told them that although I appear to be fine, she feared that I was a ticking time bomb waiting to go off. It wouldn't take much for me to become withdrawn and uncommunicative. Dr. Jill had to be the one in control. They agreed and said that if they had their way, they wouldn't discuss it at all, but knowing me as they did, they knew I would press them for answers, answers that they knew they wouldn't give. Dr. Jill asked me to join them and proceeded to give me my next appointment date. Fortunately, I was scheduled within two days just as before.

Liam told us that he had some business to attend to, so we were to go on without him. His plans seemed so mysterious. Since it was getting late, Sean took me to a cute little café called the Thatch and Thyme. The menu was simple but had several dishes to choose from. It just occurred to me that if Dr. Jill kept scheduling me for more sessions, we would be eating out a lot more than I'm used to. It has simply become part of our routine, at least for now. Sean was trying to be considerate of me, but I honestly didn't mind cooking. Then I thought, maybe he is trying to tell me that he would rather eat out than be subjected to my cooking? I feel a little insecure by that thought. I'll have to figure out a way to ask him without putting him on the spot.

Chapter 22

Session Four

I met session four with trepidation. It's hard to explain just why, but I knew we were close to a breakthrough, and I so badly wanted a positive outcome, not to mention that this whole ordeal was taking much longer than I thought it would. All that I could think of was that I must have a lot to say. I did sense a feeling of urgency for this to come to an end. We all wanted that, but I think it was more Dr. Jill's urgency than mine. Even though she didn't specifically say this to me, I had a feeling that she was growing concerned for my mental health. Giving that thought a little more attention, I came to the conclusion that Dr. Jill wouldn't waste her time or mine if it weren't very important, but she is being very cautious.

When we arrived for my appointment, Dr. Jill had just finished making notes relating to her last client's session and motioned for us to come into her office. I hadn't realized that although the actual sessions weren't all that long, Dr. Jill spent a great deal of time analyzing and evaluating information received from the current session and planning the next steps to be taken for future sessions. Her clients kept her very busy. By now, we all knew the routine so we took our previously assigned places and began session four.

I've spent so much time here I think I fell into my hypnotic state without being hypnotized! That didn't really happen, but that's what it felt like. Dr. Jill asked me if I was ready to begin. I said, "Yes."

DR. JILL. You will feel comfortable and relaxed now, and you won't feel threatened in any way. It will be as if you are telling me a story. Do you think you can do that?

ME. I think so. I'll try.

DR. JILL. During our last session, you indicated that they weren't finished with you yet. Do you know why they aren't finished with you yet?

ME. Not really. Maybe they will keep insisting that I continue translating for them, but I don't want to. I still haven't been cooperative. Maybe they want to continue punishing me. I can only guess.

DR. JILL. Translating for them?

ME. Yes, I know many languages.

DR. JILL. When you are back in the apartment with Sean, are you aware of the fact that you know many languages?

ME. No.

DR. JILL. Why do you think that you don't remember knowing different languages?

ME. I only know them when they allow me to know them. It's almost as if they can flip a switch, and there it is! It's always a different language and not always of the earthly kind.

DR. JILL. Translating doesn't seem all that difficult if you know the language. Why don't you want to translate for them?

ME. Because much of the time, they aren't being honest, and I don't know what to say in order to keep the peace. I can hear them talking among themselves, and they are saying that they are going to be misleading on purpose. They don't know that I can hear them. If I don't tell the truth, they seem to know it, so I can't just make up a story to tell them.

DR. JILL. I see. For now, we will continue on, but we might come back to revisit this subject later. Now I'd like to ask if they get angry with you only because of what you think about, or are you also verbalizing your thoughts?

ME. A little of both.

DR. JILL. Do they verbalize their communication with you?

ME. Yes, but not always.

DR. JILL. When they aren't physically speaking to you, how do they communicate with you? How do you know what they are saying or what they expect of you?

ME. Through some kind of thought transference. With telepathy, they don't have to use any words. Full thoughts and pictures are shared.

DR. JILL. Do you know if they have the ability to actually speak?

ME. Yes, they can, but it is usually only when they change from one appearance to another.

DR. JILL. I see.

ME. No, I don't want to go in there!

DR. JILL. Where don't you want to go?

ME. Into the private room.

DR. JILL. Why do they want to take you into the private room?

ME. They are discussing which one of them is going first.

DR. JILL. Going first? What are they planning?

ME. I'm not clear on that right now, but I don't think I'm going to like it much. I never do!

DR. JILL. Are they communicating with you now?

ME. No. They are arguing among themselves.

DR. JILL. Do you know what they are arguing about?

ME. I can hear only portions of their argument.

DR. JILL. Is any of it making any sense to you?

ME. No. They are arguing about some type of clause in their agreement and about something unrelated to the agreement. I can't hear much.

DR. JILL. Were you aware of an agreement that they had?

ME. Yes, but I can't tell you about it now. [*I was clearly becoming agitated and fearful.*]

DR. JILL. Are they communicating with you now?

ME. Yes.

DR. JILL. What are they saying to you?

ME. One of them told me that they had made their decision.

DR. JILL. Made a decision to do what?

ME. Made a decision as to which one will go first.

DR. JILL. Which one will go first? First to do what?

ME. To rape me! I want to leave this horrible place! [*Now I was hysterically crying and unable to move.*]

DR. JILL. [*Dr. Jill gasped but had to maintain her composure.*] All right, Princess. I know this is very difficult for you, but I'd like for you to shut them out of your mind completely, relax, take a deep breath, and go to your safe and happy place. They can't hurt you. I'd like you to continue answering some questions if you think you can. Do you think you can do that, or are you too tired to continue?

ME. I don't know. I think so. [*I was crying and covering my face with my hands.*]

DR. JILL. How many figures are in the room with you?

ME. I think four or possibly five. It's hard to tell for sure.

DR. JILL. Can you see what they look like?

ME. Yes.

DR. JILL. What do they look like?

ME. Both.

DR. JILL. Both? What do you mean by both?

ME. Men and the other mean people that I can't identify.

DR. JILL. So they are separate from one another?

ME. Yes, I think they are.

DR. JILL. Why do you think that both types of beings are there?

ME. They are working together. I'm their most frustrating project.

DR. JILL. Did they rape you the same night that they hurt your face?

ME. No.

DR. JILL. Can you tell me when it happened?

ME. [*I was crying hysterically now and scrunched up in a ball on the sofa between Sean and Liam.*] It had to be a few weeks later because my face was better. I'm not sure.

DR. JILL. We are almost done, Princess. I want you to relax and think about your happy place. When you are comfortable in your happy place can you tell me one or two more things?

ME. I'll try.

DR. JILL. Were Sean and Liam aware that you left and came back again?

ME. No.

DR. JILL. Why not?

ME. Maybe because I wasn't gone as long or maybe it happened in the middle of the night and they returned me before morning. I just can't say for sure. I don't remember. I didn't have any new cuts or bruises visibly showing when I returned so they would have no way of knowing I had gone anywhere.

DR. JILL. Were you as upset when you returned as you usually are after an episode?

ME. No. I didn't remember being gone again. They probably did something to me to make me forget their abuse just like all the other times. If there are no outward signs and if I'm not injured, I'm not aware that I've been assaulted. I didn't feel one hundred percent well for a couple of days, but I didn't know why.

DR. JILL. You are in a safe place now and relaxed. Take a deep breath. I'm going to count backward from three to one. When I reach one, you will awaken feeling refreshed and peaceful. Three, two, one. Open your eyes now, Princess.

Dr. Jill seemed a little more concerned for me than usual and asked me how I was feeling. I told her that I was glad that this session has ended. I don't feel quite as I usually do after a session. I feel a little like a knotted-up rag doll. Dr. Jill whispered that she wasn't surprised at all but assured me that I handled the session very well. She was always amazed by my strength and said that I must be a real spitfire. I wasn't exactly feeling that way just then, but I do know I'm not one that would ever allow anyone to take advantage of me.

Chapter 23

Exhaustion

Again, with a disappointing lack of information from my last session, my fifth and hopefully final session was scheduled. When we left Dr. Jill's office though, for some reason, I was feeling uncomfortable and tired, so I really wasn't in the mood to stop to eat as we usual did. But I didn't want to deny Sean and Liam the pleasure that I knew they looked forward to. They had given so much of their time and energy to my mess of a life, I could hardly say no. I didn't order much to eat. Sean seemed a little alarmed at that, but I assured him that I just wasn't all that hungry. I ate my salad and sipped my drink in silence, which was also not my norm. Sean leaned over a bit in Liam's direction and whispered, "Eat fast!" Feeling that my behavior was way off, Sean and Liam wanted to leave as soon as possible.

When we got back to the apartment, I told Sean that I needed to lay down for a bit. I desperately needed to rest my body. Apparently, my sessions were getting much more intense and leave me feeling so much more drained. I was trying to justify in my own mind the reason for my fatigue and low energy. That made more sense than anything else I could come up with. While I was resting with my eyes closed, I found it difficult to nap. As hard as I tried, I couldn't fall asleep. I was aware that Sean looked in on me often to make sure I was doing all right. Or maybe he was looking in on me to make sure

I hadn't been taken again! If that was the case, I don't know what he would have done if I really had disappeared. There's absolutely nothing that he could possibly do to stop it. He didn't seem to be himself either. There was definitely a cloud hanging over him because he didn't know about the last time I was taken from the apartment. He couldn't talk to me about it, so he had to suffer alone and in silence.

When I felt rested, I went out to join Sean. He was sitting in front of his computer in his office but looked as though he was having a hard time concentrating on work. I didn't want to disturb him, but I did want to let him know that I was up, still there and doing okay. Although he tried, he couldn't hide the fact that he was extremely concerned about me.

Rather than disturb him in his office, I decided to make a little noise in the kitchen. Coffee sounded really good anyway. Realizing that I was up and moving around, Sean walked in to the kitchen and said that the aroma of brewing coffee was calling to him. He asked if I was feeling better and more like my old self. I did feel better but definitely not my old self, so I just told him that I felt better and more rested.

We sat together at the kitchen table and started talking when out of the blue, I realized that we had never touched on the subject of his life or his childhood at all. How selfish of me. I was ashamed of myself for being so self-absorbed for the entire time that I had been there.

I decided that there was no time like the present, so in my usual, partially tactful way, I told him that I wanted to know about his childhood and about his parents and insisted that he not leave anything out. I didn't even know if he had any brothers or sisters.

He told me that he'd be more than happy to fill me in on all the details, but he still had more work to get done. That would have to come first, before anything. Right now, that was much more important than learning about his childhood. Actually, I was fine with that because I still wasn't feeling normal and resting a while longer didn't seem like a bad idea. I grabbed my coffee and a book from the bookshelf and retired to the bedroom. I wasn't particular about the book that I had chosen. Any book would do. So far, I had found every-thing in Sean's library to be excellent reading.

I made myself comfortable and looked at the book to see what I had selected. At first, from the title, I thought it was more infor-mation about Ireland, but upon closer examination, I found that it absolutely was not lighthearted reading. The book was titled *In the Woods* by Tana French. It appears to be fiction, yet it covers the very sensitive subject of child abduction. The year was 1984, and the story takes place in a small Dublin suburb during the summer months. During this time period, it was usual and customary for children to play outside until dusk. That's when the mums and dads would call their children to come back home. It seems that one night, three children didn't return home. The police did find one of the children gripping a tree trunk. He was terrorized by something, but he couldn't recall any of the details of the previous hours. The story then turns to twenty years later. The found boy, Rob Ryan, is a detective now on the Dublin Murder Squad, but he keeps his past a secret. When a twelve-year-old girl is found murdered in the same woods that he used to play in, he and his partner find themselves investigating the case, a case that is frightfully similar to the previous unsolved mystery. Detective Ryan and his partner must now solve this new mystery, and in doing so, he may uncover the mystery of his own past that he was still unable to remember. My interest has been stirred, so I'll continue reading. While I do know that it's fiction, I still feel sadness in what could be a true story. My own abuses could also be fiction, yet I know that my story is completely true.

Chapter 24

Growing Up

Approaching the subject of Sean's childhood, he said that there wasn't much to tell. His reluctance to talk about himself was apparent for the second time. Nevertheless, he continued saying that it was fairly uneventful, except for a couple of stupid things that he might have done as a teenager, with Liam of course. He didn't want to go into detail about that. I figured that since it was during his high school years, it didn't seem all that important. To my surprise, Sean told me that he is an only child. I was surprised to hear that and never would have guessed it. I never saw anything in his personality that would even suggest that as if I would know of a category to put only children in or what they would or should act like. I was an only child too! There really was no specific mold or one-size-fits-all pattern of behavior to fit that theory. Not only that, but he also shared with me the fact that he had been adopted, not as an infant, but at the age of ten. At that moment, I felt that his parents were two very special people much like my own parents were and he was extremely blessed. They were very successful at parenting as Sean was as close to being as perfect as a human being could possibly be. Sean said that they made him feel as though his home had always been with them and he knew they loved him. He didn't feel like he was just visiting or only there for a short time. He knew that this was his forever home and loved them as much as they loved him. When he was adopted, his adoptive parents told him that when the time was right, they would share some kind of letter or card with him. He was only ten years old, so he didn't think much about it at the time and eventually forgot about it. That is until today when he was recalling the events of his adoption. He didn't know about his parents though. Apparently, the time still isn't right, or they themselves have forgotten about it.

Sean's parents were both professional people but preferred living a simple life. It seems that neither of them had any desire to be influenced by or to emulate their colleagues. The cottage that they lived in was more spacious than most but was still unpretentious all the same. Living a simple life was exactly what they did, and that's what they wanted for Sean as well. He grew up learning a love of reading and an appreciation for nature and was taught to respect others as well as himself. These are just a few qualities instilled in him. Perhaps being an only child and being the focus of his parents' attention was the reason for so many of his good qualities, as well as his interest in technology. He is very good at his job.

I asked him if he regularly kept in touch with them, and he said that he usually did until I got there. I had become his priority and would remain so until my mysteries have been resolved. I was experiencing an enormous feeling of guilt because I didn't want to be the cause of them being distanced from one another. They should be continuing their relationship as if I weren't there. Sean told me that he had been in touch with them and let them know that he wouldn't be calling as much as he usually did. He didn't want them to worry and assured them that everything was fine and used his work as the excuse.

I asked about any relatives that he might have, and he told me that he didn't have any that he knew of. Both his mum and dad were also only children, so there were no aunts, uncles, or cousins. I felt sorry for him in a way. At least, I knew that I had my cousin stored in my memories and the time that we did get to spend together was always satisfying and memorable.

I still didn't feel good about this and just added it to my list of things to feel badly about. I made Sean promise me that he would get in touch with his folks after my next session, no matter what. Keeping them isolated from him wasn't fair. He promised that he would. I'll make sure that he does, and I hope at some point, he will want to include me. Right now though, the important thing is for him to continue with the same relationship that he's always had with them.

In my mind, for some reason, I thought he and Liam had been friends since meeting when they were ten years of age. Obviously, that wasn't the case. During his secondary school years, Sean was exposed to a superior education. His parents found a school that not only taught the general subjects but also exposed him to a much more technological curriculum. He always excelled in his under-standing of the newest technology. It was there that Sean and Liam met. Although they were total opposites in personality, they imme-diately connected and hit it off. They've been best friends since then. They learned as much about each other as they possibly could. After so many years as best friends, they almost seem to know what the other was thinking. Now, I was wondering why Liam never brought up their past. I can only surmise that he and Sean had talked among themselves and decided that the focus should be on me, at least for the time being. I hoped that wasn't the case. I was already feeling guilty enough.

Chapter 25

Session Five

I was desperately hoping that session five would be my last and knew that we would be finding out very soon. It seemed as though each new session was more wearing and exhausting than the one before. I knew that Dr. Jill, Sean, and Liam could see it too, but I now know that they had agreed to keep their feelings hidden from me. If the intensity of my sessions increased at all, Dr. Jill was afraid that my mental well-being would be at great risk regardless of my strength and desire to know the truth. All she could do was evaluate each session based on its own merits. As a professional, she would know when or if it was time to back off.

Arriving right on time, Dr. Jill was waiting in her office. As we entered her office, we proceeded to take our usual seats. I noticed that a second chair had been positioned next to her chair. Me being me, I was the first to question her. "Are we expecting company," I asked.

She said, "No, no company coming."

"Then what is the second chair for?" I asked. She told me to take a seat in the chair next to hers. I wasn't at all sure that I was comfortable with that arrangement, but I did trust her judgment. Being so far away from Sean and Liam for the first time was a little unsettling. It felt unnatural and really odd to me.

As I made myself comfortable in the chair, sitting on my legs as I usually did, she proceeded to put me into that increasingly familiar trance.

Once she was absolutely sure I was under her control, she started questioning me again.

Dr. Jill. Are you comfortable and ready to begin?

Me. Yes.

Dr. Jill. During your last session, you mentioned an agreement that was made between both parties. I'd like to know more about this agreement. I want you to focus only on the agreement and tell me what agreement was made. Can you do that?

Me. Yes, I think I can do that.

Dr. Jill. Why don't you just convey to me what you think this agreement is about. Start at whatever point you are most comfortable with.

Me. At first, I was thinking I was part of some kind of secret program.

Dr. Jill. What kind of program?

Me. You know, the kind of program that the government hides from the public for years and years before admitting that there is indeed such a program.

Dr. Jill. Why did you think that?

Me. Because I was already aware of other hidden, secret programs that the government was involved in, so I thought this was just a new one that they came up with.

Dr. Jill. Do you still feel that way?

Me. No.

Dr. Jill. Do you think that this agreement was made just for you?

Me. For me and others like me.

Dr. Jill. Others like you?

Me. Yes, like me.

Dr. Jill. Like you in what way? What do you mean?

Me. Having the ability to remember things that I see and hear.

Dr. Jill. Doesn't everybody have that ability?

Me. Not at all.

Dr. Jill. Why do you think you have that special ability?

ME. Because I and a few others are different.

DR. JILL. Different in what way?

ME. We are different because of our intelligence level.

DR. JILL. I'd like to go back to the actual agreement. Is that all right with you?

ME. Yes, but they're watching me.

DR. JILL. Can you give me some specifics about the agreement?

ME. I have to be careful. They are still watching me and monitoring what I think and say. The agreement isn't all that long. It has maybe two stipulations, but they are very important. Even though it's called an agreement, to me, it's more like a treaty, the kind that can't be broken.

DR. JILL. Will you tell me the details of this treaty?

ME. I want to, but I can't right now. Oh no! They are coming toward me. I have to leave. I have to leave! It's not safe.

DR. JILL. I want you to relax, take a deep breath, and go to your safe space.

ME. I can't this time!

DR. JILL. Why not? Why can't you go to your safe space?

ME. Because they took it from me. I don't have a place to hide any more.

DR. JILL. I'm going to reach over and touch your hand. When I do, you will immediately feel a calm that you've never felt before. You'll know that you can't be harmed in any way as long as my hand is touching yours. I'm touching your hand now. Can you feel my touch?

ME. Yes.

DR. JILL. How are you feeling now?

ME. Wonderful and so at peace.

DR. JILL. Good. [*With her hand still touching my hand*] I'm going to count backward from three to one. When I reach the number one, you will wake up and open your eyes. Three, two, one.

"Are you feeling calm and relaxed now?" Dr. Jill asked. Absolutely, I feel like me! Apparently we won't need a session number six, right? Can you fill me in on everything now? At the risk of my throwing a tantrum and stomping out, Dr. Jill said that we would definitely need a session six and she couldn't tell me anything about this session.

She was right to be concerned because the look on my face said, "I don't like you anymore, I'm not putting up with this any longer, and I don't want to continue on!" Dr. Jill reached over and touched the top of my hand, and before I knew it, I had totally agreed to another session.

All seems well with the world, and I said, "Well, if we're done for now, I'm thinking that I really need something to eat. Would you like to join us, Dr. Jill?" Dr. Jill responded that she'd love to but it would have to be another time. She had one more appointment before she could end her day. A sixth session appointment was made before we left though.

Chapter 26

A Surprising Calm

My feeling happy and content and hungry left Sean and Liam completely confused. They were glad to see that I was back to myself but really confused none the less. They could see how agitated I was before Dr. Jill touched the top of my hand. What had just happened? Whatever it was, why did that make such a difference? It was a mystery to them and was just all too easy. I was too willing to do as she asked without being combative. Sean and Liam discussed it later and concluded that it must have been an unnoticed posthypnotic suggestion on Dr. Jill's part.

At lunch, I even ordered a glass of wine. Normally, I don't drink during the day. It was just a little something else to confuse them, but they weren't questioning it. They thought it would be best to take things as they came and go with the flow. Our lunch was long and was leisurely eaten. When we were finished, Sean asked me if there was anything in particular that I'd like to do. We still had the rest of the afternoon to goof off, and since I seemed to be back to my old self, there was no need to rush back to the apartment. Liam jumped in and said that he had a great idea. Sean and I just looked at each other because we'd seen that look before. It usually meant trouble. Surprisingly, it actually sounded like a fun way to spend the afternoon. Liam knew of an arcade with everything from shuffle board to pinball and some amusement park attractions. If we couldn't find anything that we liked to do there, we wouldn't find it anywhere. I have to admit that I had a wonderful time. I don't think I've been to a place like that since my high school days. Sean seemed impressed with Liam's suggestion as well. I know that the little boys inside these two guys were begging to be set free! I was surprised that two grown men knew how to play almost every single arcade game. We were all getting tired and were starting to show that we weren't kids any more, not that we're old by any stretch of the imagination. It was time to drop Liam at his place and for us to head home.

Without saying a word, Sean and I both knew that we wouldn't want another meal again until tomorrow. It seems as though all we do is eat! It felt good to get into our comfy clothes and crash on the sofa. Sean remembered taping a movie that we were both interested in seeing. Within a minute, he was pushing the play button on the remote. We were settled in for the night.

I was so tired I could barely finish watching the movie. I think I was in bed before Sean could turn off the TV. It didn't take him long to follow behind me. He kissed me goodnight and was snoring before I could even turn to my favorite side.

Morning greeted us with tons of sun pouring in, and it was a treat to see it. Even though the month isn't over, most days that I've experienced are usually overcast and gloomy or downright wet from rain, not today though, and sunshine always puts me in a good mood. Sean and I sat at the table enjoying our coffee and this beautiful day.

After our second cup, Sean said that he needed to get some work done. He gave me a kiss on the forehead and said, "You know where to find me if you need me for anything." He wasn't the only one who needed to get things done today. Having the afternoon yesterday to do nothing but goof off and have fun was great, but it was time to get back to reality and responsibility.

Chapter 27

Liam's Visits

Our dinner conversation was usually about Sean's work or any plans that we might be looking forward to. I was still redecorating that cottage in my head. It was fun thinking about it, but my mind quickly changed gears. This time, Liam was the one invading the thoughts that were bouncing around in my head. I looked over at Sean and said, "Have you noticed that Liam hasn't been randomly stopping by as much as he used to?"

Sean said, "As a matter of fact, I did notice that." I asked Sean if he had any notion as to why that was. Sean told me that he couldn't say for sure but that he suspected that there might be someone special in Liam's life at the moment. Liam hadn't mentioned anything to Sean yet, but Sean had already decided to question him the next time they had a boy's night out.

I told him to plan one soon because I was dying to know. "Aren't you curious, Sean?" I asked.

He said, "No, not really. I figured he would tell me when he was ready. Besides, Liam's relationships don't usually last very long. I love him like a brother, but he is not as flexible as he could be. He may have improved in that area though." I asked him why he thought that might be. Sean said that he's noticed a difference in Liam since my arrival here. He seems ready and willing to do whatever we need

115

him to do, when we need it, which is definitely not like Liam. I told Sean that I really did have a special place in my heart for Liam, just as he did.

I had totally forgotten to ask Sean if he had gotten in touch with his parents after my fifth session as promised. When I finally got around to asking him, he told me that he has called them at least twice since then. I know that Sean is a man of his word and deep down I couldn't imagine him not keeping his promise. I was surprised but definitely happy to hear that he told them about me. He didn't tell them everything of course. How could he? In their last conversation, they asked him what my name was. He and Liam had been calling me Princess for so long he couldn't imagine calling me by any other name. He said that he matter-of-factly told them that my name was Princess. He was expecting them to say that they thought it was an odd name, but they didn't. He said that they actually liked it and thought it was unique. He was so relieved.

Much to my surprise, Sean had discussed the possibility of paying them a visit. The drive wasn't terribly long, and a long weekend was approaching because of an Irish holiday. The October Bank Holiday was on the last Monday of October. I had never heard of it, but Sean explained that it was first marked in 1977 after the Irish government determined that the holiday would be a welcome break after the long stretch of time between summer and Christmas. In my excitement and wanting to meet his parents, I begged him to go, just as a little kid would. He told me to stop begging because he had already decided we would go if that's what I wanted to do.

"It's settled then. I do want to go so just tell me when to be ready, and I'll be waiting at the door for you."

Sean said, "It sounds like you are more than ready for a change of pace."

"Yes, I am, can you blame me? Actually, it's not just that I need a change of pace. I also looked forward to meeting your parents."

Chapter 28

Session Six

Dr. Jill seemed as anxious as we were to learn more about me, not that I was privy to much information at this point. I think I'm getting used to it now, and I pretty much expect her to tell me to be patient.

At any rate, we were there right on time, and Dr. Jill was ready and waiting for us. Even though we knew the drill by now, she motioned to us to take our seats, the same as my last session. Dr. Jill wanted me to sit next to her as I had done for the previous session. I think that she felt she had more control if I reacted badly to her questions. We sat down, and before I knew it, I was in a hypnotic trance.

DR. JILL. Are you ready to begin, Princess?

ME. Yes, I'm ready.

DR. JILL. Early on, you said that they had the ability to remove memories. Can they remove all memories or just some memories?

ME. For most people, they remove only those memories of being taken, hurt, or abused in some way. They don't normally leave any telltale signs of bruises or cuts or scratches. That way, their victims don't even know that anything happened to them. For others, at times, they find it necessary to remove all memories associated with the event. If they feel that someone will remember even the smallest detail or trauma, they just erase it. They can't risk making a mistake.

DR. JILL. If they can remove all memories when they want to, why didn't they remove all your memories? Wouldn't they view you as less of a threat to them?

ME. I'm sure they would, but they aren't allowed to.

DR. JILL. Who won't allow them to do what they want?

ME. Not who, but what.

DR. JILL. All right then, what keeps them from doing what they want to do?

ME. The agreement that they signed.

DR. JILL. What exactly is in the agreement that keeps them from doing what they want?

ME. They agreed to limit their control and power over people like me. They are specifically forbidden to erase all our memories. There will be serious consequences if they go back on their word.

DR. JILL. What would those consequences be?

ME. I don't know. As far as I know, they have never broken their word. I don't think that even they know what those consequences are, and they don't want to find out.

DR. JILL. I'd like to know a little more about the agreement, or treaty as you put it. You said that it was for people like you. What makes you special or different?

ME. I am a hybrid.

DR. JILL. [Dr. Jill is momentarily left breathless and speechless.] Did I hear you correctly? You are a hybrid?

ME. Yes, I am a hybrid.

DR. JILL. Can you tell me what a hybrid is?

ME. A hybrid is a person that has human and alien DNA.

DR. JILL. I see. So why aren't they allowed to control the brain and all memories of a hybrid?

ME. Because, as an experiment, we are far too valuable to them. They aren't allowed to risk permanently hurting us in any way. I think that they have taken me pretty much to the limits allowed. I already have scars on my back, and any further abuse might possibly hurt me permanently.

DR. JILL. That's a good sign, don't you think?

ME. Considering that they aren't done with me yet, I would have to agree. What else could they possibly do?

DR. JILL. Can you tell me about your hybrid parents?

ME. My mother was a human, but I also have the DNA of several different species of aliens.

DR. JILL. Do you know the race of your most predominant alien DNA?

ME. I think it's Arcturian. They can exist in many forms, but the main race is about five feet tall with a greenish skin and large eyes.

DR. JILL. Why then do you look and act totally like a human?

ME. Because my genetics and DNA have shown that I am of my mother by a much greater percentage than anything else. I share very few alien characteristics. I share alien intellect and nothing more.

DR. JILL. I always thought that genetics and DNA were shared equally from both parents.

ME. Not when you are a hybrid.

DR. JILL. Do you know who or where your birth mother is?

ME. No. Knowing those details is permitted only on very rare occasions, under special circumstances.

DR. JILL. Do you know if your adoptive parents were both humans?

ME. Yes, they were.

DR. JILL. Why do you remember having human parents?

ME. Because I remember being adopted by them and I remember that I felt loved and wanted.

DR. JILL. Do you know who your human parents are?

ME. No, that's one of the memories they don't want me to have. If I had an awareness of who they were, then I could research who I am and where I come from. Any memories I might have that could possibly lead me to my own identity must remain hidden at all cost.

DR. JILL. Did your parents adopt you as an infant?

ME. No. I was adopted as an older child.

DR. JILL. Do you remember how old you were when you were adopted?

ME. Not exactly. I think that I was around ten years old.

DR. JILL. Did they share any of the details of your adoption with you?

ME. Only that they were extremely excited about being my mom and dad. They said that they would answer any questions I might have when the time was right.

DR. JILL. Did you ever feel that the time was right to ask questions?

ME. No. I never felt the need to know anything outside of our own family.

DR. JILL. Did you go to a regular school with regular kids?

ME. Yes, but I was taking advanced classes throughout grammar and high school. I remember that in high school, I did take some college courses related to my field of interest.

DR. JILL. What was your field of interest?

ME. They don't want me to remember that.

DR. JILL. After high school, did you go to college?

ME. Yes.

DR. JILL. Where did you go to college?

ME. I don't know. They won't allow me to have that memory either.

DR. JILL. You're doing really well, Princess. Are you willing to continue, or are you tired?

ME. No, I don't want to continue now. They are watching me again. I need to stop.

DR. JILL. I understand. [*Dr. Jill reached over with her caring hand and gently touched the top of my mine.*] I'm going to count backward from three to one. When I reach the number one, you will wake up feeling refreshed and open your eyes. Three, two, one.

Dr. Jill asked me how I was feeling, and I told her that I never felt better. She indicated that she was happy to hear that because we would be having another session and she wasn't sure how she was going to break it to me. She asked me to be patient just a short while longer. She confirmed that all my sessions were revealing a great deal about me, but when the time was right, she wanted to tell my whole story. Giving me just fragments would probably just confuse me. She told me that she had a complete understanding of my story and asked that I trust her a little while longer. Now my seventh session was noted in her appointment book.

I was asked once again to take a seat in the outer waiting room, but this time, Sean was the one making the request. I looked at him and said, "Seriously?"

He gave me a hug and whispered that it would only take a minute and said, "Please, for me." I didn't want to, but he was so nice and polite about it, I could hardly say no. Liam said that he would sit with me until Sean was finished.

Now, Sean was alone with Dr. Jill and felt that he had to address something that I had said while being questioned. He went on to tell her that he wasn't sure at all if it actually had any significance. He said it might be nothing but then again it might be something. Dr. Jill told him to let her be the judge of that. Sean went on to say that obviously, "When she said that she was a hybrid, I nearly fainted, but when she said that she had been adopted at around the age of ten, I was stunned. I wasn't aware of that she had been adopted. I was totally blown away!"

Dr. Jill asked Sean why he was so astonished at my being adopted. After all, adoption was a perfectly natural occurrence, at any age.

Sean said, "I was also adopted at ten years of age. She just recently became aware of my adoption after asking about my childhood. The similarities are uncanny, and it's hard to wrap my head around that. Either she was influenced by my childhood story and carried it over to this session, or there truly are similarities. I just don't know."

Dr. Jill told Sean that she wanted to pursue this conversation further, but if we take the time now, I would become suspicious and wonder what's taking so long. Sean agreed, and they ended the conversation, but Dr. Jill did say that she would be reaching out to him for further discussion very soon.

Chapter 29

Mrs. MacDonald's Long Wait

We followed our usual routine, but Liam didn't join us. He was extremely vague in his description of his afternoon plans. Liam certainly didn't owe us any explanation, but he was always so willing to share everything with us. Sometimes he would share even more than we cared to know. We didn't mind though because we knew it was just Liam being Liam.

When we arrived home, it was later in the afternoon, and of course, Mrs. MacDonald was sitting on the lower step of the landing, waiting for Sean to be her knight in shining armor again. Of course, we were both ready and willing to help out with whatever was needed. I asked her if she had been waiting long, and she said, "Well, I don't really know. A couple of other people in the building asked if I needed help, but I told them that I was waiting for Sean." I could hardly believe what I was hearing. Sean really is her "go to" guy! It seems that she nodded off for a few minutes while sitting on the stairs. Bless her little heart, she can even sleep on those hard stairs. I kept wondering what her bed must be like. At any rate, Sean seemed to fill her needs quite nicely until the next time.

Sean wanted to talk about my session with Dr. Jill so badly, but he knew that he couldn't. He would never do anything to jeopardize Dr. Jill's accomplishments or my well-being. All he could do was to be patient, just as I had to do. Since I wasn't aware of his concerns, I had no way of knowing that he was on pins and needles. He hid it well though because I didn't have a clue that he was anxious about anything.

We hadn't made any plans for that evening, and we had already watched a movie the night before, so I asked Sean if he had any board games. He said he had a Scrabble game. I jumped at the chance to play a game of Scrabble. I hadn't played in a very long time, but I absolutely adore word games. It didn't take long for him to figure out that he had met his match. For every good word he came up with, I came up with an even better one. I started feeling sorry for him and almost gave in to letting him win. Then I thought better of it. He wouldn't want to win if it wasn't fair and square. At just about three quarters of the way into our game, the phone in his office rang. He answered it but wasn't gone very long. He told me that a client needed to meet with him and asked him if he was available tomorrow. He always had work to do but not so much that he couldn't rearrange his schedule, so they set up a time to meet. We finished our game, which by the way, I ended up winning. I'm surely no genius, but it appears that my vocabulary is quite extensive. Sean went through his nightly routine and met me in the bedroom.

As we were lying there, just talking, I turned to him and whispered, "I love you so very much." I wasn't planning that at all. It fell out of my mouth so unexpectedly. I think that I was as shocked as he was. His eye widened a little, and he just looked at me with a brief stare. I felt nothing but relief when he leaned over and kissed me passionately.

He said, "I love you too, very much." We both enjoyed the kissing and love making. I wanted it to last all night, but I knew that it couldn't. We fell asleep lying near each other as closely as possible and woke the next morning still wrapped in each other's arms. This is what loving someone is supposed to feel like. Oh, I know there's so much more to loving than just a great physical relationship, but I felt so blessed to be experiencing all of it.

Since Sean needed to work away from the apartment today, I decided it would be a good time to read more of that fascinating book. It was so suspenseful but at times so sad. Finding that the story made me feel melancholy, I found the book so hard to put down. I think I was identifying with the abducted children. Somehow, I could relate to them and knew what they were thinking and what they were feeling. It was surreal, and yet it was familiar to me. How very sad for those poor children who never returned. I can't even begin to imagine how or why a parent would want to go on living if they were never to know what happened to them. For a moment, I was grateful that my own parents weren't on this earth any more. They would never have a way of knowing what happened to me, and I know it would be devastating for them.

Chapter 30

The Appointment

Sean showered and prepared for that unexpected client appointment. Finding that he had plenty of time to spare, he did enjoy a cup of coffee with me. We always liked our mornings together, which always seemed to fly by way too fast. Sean kissed me on the forehead and said it was time for him to leave, but he didn't seem as excited as he usually is. I didn't give it much thought though. He told me that he didn't anticipate being longer than an hour and a half or so, but if he ended up being gone longer than that, I wasn't to worry. I know that he was uneasy about leaving me alone for any length of time. The memory of coming home to a quiet apartment, only to find that I was gone, played over and over in his mind.

I found quite a lot to keep me busy, and I knew that I still had to plan our dinner. We usually didn't eat early, so I had more than enough time to prepare a Crock-Pot meal. Sean liked anything coming from a Crock-Pot. I have to admit, he was pretty easy to please, and as it turns out, he does like my cooking.

Although I didn't know it, Sean's unexpected meeting was with Dr. Jill. She was the one who had called the evening before. She wanted to aggressively pursue the conversation that Sean had started in her office after my session. She was anxious to know if he had any specific thoughts about his concerns and wanted to know more. Dr.

Jill was so intrigued by their adoptions being so similar but agreed that I may have been influenced by Sean's childhood. There was only one way to find out. She asked if Sean would be agreeable to being hypnotized and suggested that it may be the key in solving some of the mystery. While she did have some thoughts about it, she wanted to be absolutely sure that she was on the right track, or she would find out that she was heading in the wrong direction. Sean squirmed in his seat for a few minutes and tried to avoid her suggestion. Dr. Jill was patient long enough, and now she felt that she had to push Sean to give her a straight answer. She asked him if he was afraid to be hypnotized. He said that the thought never occurred to him. He indicated that he was somewhat uncomfortable being another one of her subjects. Dr. Jill assured him that her questions would only address the subject at hand and nothing else. Reluctantly, Sean agreed.

Dr. Jill asked Sean to sit on the sofa across from her, and she easily transitioned him into a hypnotic trance and began with her questions. Her entire line of questioning concerned only his adoption, childhood, parents, and education. They were finished within about forty-five minutes. Sean awoke feeling refreshed and normal. Dr. Jill told him that she felt that they were going in the right direction. Sean wanted to know more about the session just as I did after my sessions, but Dr. Jill felt that the results of her final evaluation should be shared at the very end, the very end being when she has decided that further sessions were no longer needed. Needless to say, Sean wasn't happy with that arrangement, but he had already agreed to do whatever Dr. Jill deemed necessary.

As Sean was leaving Dr. Jill's office, he phoned Liam and asked him if he was available to meet for a beer. Liam would never turn down a chance to down a cold one, and Sean knew that. They agreed to meet at their favorite pub. Sean wanted to tell Liam what had just happened. He had to tell someone, and he knew he couldn't tell me. While they were enjoying some guy time together, Sean told his story and asked Liam what he thought about his being hypnotized. Liam didn't know quite what to say. Scratching his head, he said, "Man, you're one brave, dude. I don't think I could have done it."

Sean said, "Not even for Princess?" Liam had to admit that he would if it helped their Princess. Of course, Liam didn't know anything about the earlier conversation that Sean had with Dr. Jill. Liam was very much aware of the circumstances of Sean's adoption, but he hadn't given it a second thought. Sean seemed to be more in tune with that sort of thing. Liam was always the happy go lucky guy, and Sean was always a fun guy but more reserved and a little more serious. That's probably why they got along so well and became the friends that they are.

The two of them had finished their conversation about Sean's somewhat weird adventure, and Sean figured it was a good time to approach Liam about possibly having a new friend in his life. I honestly think that he was just as anxious to know as I was. Liam had never been quite that secretive with Sean about such things, but this time was different.

Sean asked Liam why he hadn't been around as much as he usually was. He explained that he was only being a friend and not being intrusive but that he did have a theory. Liam looked at Sean and said, "I can just imagine what your theory is! Yes, I have been seeing a certain young lady. That's your theory, right?" Sean said yes and asked Liam for all of the juicy details because he knew that I was dying to know! Liam was only too happy to brag on his manhood and proceeded to tell Sean about this beautiful woman he had met. Her name was Hannah which he found to be just as beautiful as the rest of her. He went on and on about her beautiful brunette hair, her china-like skin, her curvy figure, and anything else he could think of that described her exterior looks.

Sean just stared at Liam for a minute and said, "Liam!!! You do know that there is a lot more to a relationship than looks, right?" Being beautiful was always what Liam would notice first. The other stuff didn't seem all that important to him. That's probably why his relationships didn't last long. Liam told Sean that he was beginning to see more than just beauty. It seems that since he had been watching the interaction between Sean and me, he decided that he should pay closer attention to what's on the inside too. He told Sean exactly that, and Sean agreed that at least it was a step in the right direction.

Sean told Liam he had only one more question and asked him if he would promise to give him an honest, truthful answer.

Liam agreed and said, "Go ahead. Shoot. I'm ready for anything."

Sean said, "Please tell me she isn't married! Is she married?" From the look on Liam's face, he was ready for any question but that one! As he started his answer with the word well, followed by, "You see," Sean just cringed. He told Liam that he really wasn't ready to hear more and that he should be very careful. Having a husband in the picture is not a good thing. The guys finished their drinks and went their separate ways. Liam promised to keep in touch more often and that he would keep Sean in his romantic loop.

Chapter 31

Perception

When Sean walked in from his appointment, he didn't immediately see me, and the apartment was pretty quiet. He frantically shouted out my name. Much to his relief, I ran into the living room where he was standing. With widened eyes, I said, "What? What happened?" He just hugged me and said that he was glad to see me there. Further words weren't needed.

Not knowing much about Sean's appointment, I was anxious to hear all about it. He was usually excited about having client meetings, but this meeting seemed different. I just figured the appointment was with his newest client that he had signed with only a short time ago. When he walked in, I told him that I was anxious to hear about his day and that we needed to sit over coffee so he could tell me absolutely everything. I thought that it was important that I continue to show my genuine interest in his work, and I really did want to know everything. He always made his job sound so interesting.

As we sat at the kitchen table, he proceeded to tell me that his meeting was with his newest client. He seemed confused and rattled in his explanation, but I didn't want to push it. He's not very good at making up stories. Something was going on, but I had no idea what it was.

I mentioned that I thought it was a really long meeting. He said, "Oh, I almost forgot. I met Liam, and we had a couple of beers." Now that made a lot more sense to me. Sitting straighter and more upright in my chair with my hands clasped under my chin, I smiled and told Sean that I was excited and anxious to hear what Liam had to say. I knew that Sean surely would have asked Liam why he hadn't been visiting as often as he usually did. Sean told me that he did bring up the subject and Liam was fairly open about it. It seems that he does have a new love interest in his life. In my excitement for Liam having a relationship, I told Sean how pleased and happy I was for him. Sean said, "Just hold on a minute. I think we should just wait and see what happens and see if the relationship progresses." At first, he seemed a little secretive, but then he told me everything. I agreed that maybe I was jumping to conclusions, but due to his hesitation, I had to ask if there might be something that he was purposely leaving out. Sean chuckled under his breath and said, "You know me too well."

I said, "All right, buster, it's time to tell the rest of the story." Sean said that there wasn't much more other than the fact that his new friend was married. I almost fell off my chair. I had no words at first. After about a minute, I found myself ranting and raving about it and asking Sean if Liam was totally out of his mind. I knew that Liam was more flighty than Sean but this! Really? I would never have guessed that in a million years.

Sean said that in the past, Liam usually took the safe route, the route that allows him the luxury of not committing. He just hasn't broken that pattern yet. Sean said, "I do believe that he will though. When he sees us together, he is reminded that he wants that same kind of relationship. It's just a matter of time, and he'll find that right someone."

Being distracted by Liam's so-called love life made me forget about the business appointment that Sean had earlier. It wasn't until later that night that I started thinking about it again. I didn't pursue it any further, but something still felt off, and I couldn't shake the feeling that something was wrong. It just wasn't like Sean to be so vague about his clients. The truth be told, sometimes, he tells me a whole lot more that I really need to know, but not this time. If it happens again, I'll know for sure that something really is wrong. Until then, I'll give him the benefit of the doubt and just try to forget about it.

My thoughts turned to Liam again. I actually was frightened for him. I've seen what can happen too many times not to know that when you play with matches, you usually get burned. And to me, it looked like that's where he was headed. This situation became a double-edged sword for me. If I approach Liam about it, he might not appreciate my opinion and might think I'm butting in, and he'll just pull farther away from us. Knowing that Sean would tell me everything, if I don't say anything at all, he might think that I don't care enough to take an interest in him.

How odd! How did I know that I had seen that situation before and what the results could be too many times? Somehow a memory must have been sparked. I started searching through my memory bank to see if I had even the slightest clue, but I came up with nothing. It must have been significant at some point in my life. I had so many problems of my own right now, focusing on Liam was more than I could handle. Wading through my life with Dr. Jill and still not having a definitive answer concerning my name and where I am from was foremost on my mind. Perhaps there will be so much more brought to the surface in my next session.

Chapter 32

---— ⁓ —---

Session Seven

For some strange reason, Sean seemed to be dragging his feet a little. He's always so prompt and ready to go, but today is different. He almost seems bothered about something but insists that it's just my imagination because I'm getting tired of always having to agree to more sessions. He could be right, but it sure didn't feel like it. We finally picked up Liam and headed to Dr. Jill's office. Surprisingly, we weren't late, but if I hadn't pushed, we would have been. That in itself really bothered me. I didn't ask about it anymore because Sean was clearly annoyed and bothered by something. He just wasn't willing to share it with me. This is the first time he hadn't been completely honest with me. We've always been open and above board with everything. Why not now?

As usual, Dr. Jill was right on schedule and expecting us. She went through the usual routine. We sat in our usual places, but this time, she asked Sean to take a seat next to her. Liam and I just looked at each other in disbelief. Liam knew it must have had something to do with Sean being hypnotized, but I was totally in the dark. Before I could count to ten, Dr. Jill had put me into that familiar hypnotic state.

DR. JILL. Are you comfortable and ready to start, Princess?

Me. No!

Dr. Jill. Why aren't you ready to start today?

Me. I'm not sure. My thoughts are cloudy.

Dr. Jill. If we start, perhaps the clouds will clear up, and you won't be so apprehensive. Should we start now?

Me. I suppose.

Dr. Jill. I promise that this session will be over very quickly. In your last session, you talked about your being adopted later, as a child of about ten.

Me. Yes.

Dr. Jill. Do you remember where you went to school before being adopted?

Me. I don't remember the name of it, but I went to school with other kids like me.

Dr. Jill. So it was a special school for hybrid children only.

Me. Yes.

Dr. Jill. Are all hybrid children sent to a special school?

Me. Yes, as far as I know.

Dr. Jill. Are all hybrid children adopted?

Me. Yes, usually.

Dr. Jill. Are hybrid children ever adopted as infants?

Me. Yes, on occasion.

Dr. Jill. Why are they adopted as infants rather than at an older age like you were?

Me. Because they aren't particularly special. They don't have special talents or increased intellect.

Dr. Jill. Did your human adoptive parents know that you were a hybrid?

Me. No, I don't think so, but I can't say for sure. I think that they just thought I was really smart.

Dr. Jill. One last question. Did your adoptive parents ever tell you that they had something to share with you when the time was right?

Me. No. They said I could ask questions and that they would answer me when the time was right if they could.

Dr. Jill. As an adult, were you friends with any other hybrids?

ME. Possibly but I can't say for sure because of my memory issues.

DR. JILL. Well, Princess, I think we've looked into every aspect of your life that's important, and I've learned everything that I can. When this session is completed, you will feel refreshed and happy. I am going to count backward from three to one. When I reach one, you will awaken and open your eyes. Three, two, one.

After waking up, I had the incredible feeling that there would be no more sessions and asked Dr. Jill if I was just dreaming or if she had indeed indicated that there would be no need to go any further. She was more than happy to announce that I wasn't dreaming. She said that now, finally, I would learn everything about every session. I was still curious though. I asked her why Sean was sitting next to her instead of me. She said that she would tell us later on in the conversation.

Knowing that this could possibly be a lengthy conversation, before getting started, she offered us coffee, tea, or water so that we would be comfortable. Liam and I sat across from her while Sean sat in the chair next to her, and she was ready to start.

Chapter 33

Summary of Session One

Dr. Jill proceeded to summarize session number one. She told us that after each summary, she would give us the original tape of the actual session.

She said that she was not going to go over each tape word for word but would do her best to cover the most pertinent parts. After hearing that, I knew that I could go back to review the tapes myself later on, whenever I felt the need for clarification. At any time during her summary, if I felt the need to ask questions, I was encouraged to stop her. She reminded Sean and Liam that they already knew the content of my sessions but they were also welcome to ask questions as well. That would be far easier than stopping the tape every time we had questions.

Starting with Session One, Dr. Jill said that after summarizing each tape, she would address only that tape before moving on to the next. Now the defining moment was about to commence. Dr. Jill told me that I had been taken to an unknown location in order to be studied. I asked why, and she told me that she would be getting to that and I would have a better understanding later on. She said, "The injuries that you received were given to you as a punishment."

I said, "Stop, Dr. Jill. Why was I being punished? Did I do something horrible?"

Dr. Jill assured me that I didn't do anything horrible and wasn't a bad person but I would learn more as we progressed further. "If you'll be patient, you'll hear the answers to most of the questions that you have." She said that this is a great example of why she couldn't share information with me after each session. "At times, a following session would answer questions asked in the previous session. You were asked to describe your abductors, and you said that they seemed to be tall but that they were hard to see because of the light that was above you. You became anxious because they were standing over you. Since they were closer to you, I asked you if you could see them better in order to describe them better. You said that they looked like men, but at this point, you were anxious and afraid because they seemed angry with you. You said that they were dangerous. I asked if they were angry with only you, and you said yes, only you because you were so hard to handle and you wouldn't cooperate with them. I asked you if you could see anything else, and you said, 'Many people, just lying on tables of some sort.'"

I said, "Dr. Jill, I'm confused by something. Am I to believe that someone abducted me? Who abducted me and why?"

Dr. Jill said that those questions would be answered in later tapes and that giving me that information now would just confuse me. She said that we were going to hear one summary at a time but the complete story would come to light by the end of session seven. She apologized for encouraging me to ask questions and now knows that all my questions are valid, but they just can't be answered until we reach that level.

After digesting what I could of Session One, we proceeded with Session Two. Dr. Jill said that she took me back to the time Sean found me crouched in the corner. She asked where I was taken, but that I still wasn't sure. "You said the room was filled with computers but no windows. You called your abductors monsters and said that they were ugly and mean and that they didn't feel emotions. At that point, you told me that you were different because you had an echoic and eidetic memory and indicated that they were afraid of that. You were very stubborn and refused to do what they wanted because they wanted to manipulate you, but your resistance always resulted in your being physically abused and that was frightening. They were determined to make you a victim rather than a study subject and also make you an example of what not to do should any of the others get any similar ideas. Apparently. they had put you into some type of restraint at times because they wanted to poke and prod your body, but you stressed that your brain was the primary interest to them. They couldn't remove all your memories, and because of that, you were a threat to them. They feared being exposed by you. They always know what you are thinking. and very often, they don't like what you are thinking."

I stopped Dr. Jill for a few minutes and told her that this was all so incredible. It was almost impossible to believe. Dr. Jill agreed and said that she had a hard time believing it at first too. Sean never took his eyes off me. He was watching my reactions and making sure that I was all right. At this point, I told Dr. Jill that I was taken aback by some of her summary and I wasn't sure if I wanted to hear more. She said that we could stop for the day and continue at another time, but I found that even though I was shocked by what I was hearing, I was beyond curious and needed to know more even though I might be fearful of it. I convinced myself that although so much of it was shocking, it wasn't as shocking as the actual abuse that I suffered. I asked her to please continue on to Session Three.

She agreed and summarized Session Three and said that she started by asking me exactly what I was thinking that made them so angry and said that I told her that I kept thinking that they were changing. "You thought that they were changing appearance to confuse you. I asked you why just a simple idea would make them mad, and you told me it was because they were afraid you were getting too close to seeing their real identities." The more Dr. Jill covered, the more my interest was peaked, and I could hardly wait to find out what comes next. Dr. Jill continued and said that sometimes they looked like men but often they didn't. "They didn't look human and seemed to have a totally different appearance. You told me that they viewed human's intellect as inferior to them, but humans were somewhat intelligent." She told me that I made her quietly laugh when I said that they viewed some humans as being morons but there were some who were highly intelligent like me. "I asked you what you meant by the 'like me' comment, but you couldn't tell me because you were being watched."

Now my curiosity is getting the better of me. I was trying so hard to be patient, but I needed to know what I meant by "like me." It was going to take a while before she would get to that, and it was killing me. She changed the subject and asked if they always kept everything out in the open, and I didn't hesitate to say, "No, they have private rooms where they do horrible, unspeakable things." She said the hardest thing for her to hear at that point was that I said that they weren't finished with me yet. Knowing what I had already been through, she was overwhelmed to hear that they needed more from me. She said, "This is the hardest part of my job. I'm not allowed to react during a session, but later, when I reviewed the tapes, I was overcome with sadness and disbelief."

Hearing that was hard for me too. What could they possibly do that they haven't already done? Due to the hour and knowing that there was so much more to review, Dr. Jill asked if we would return the following day at 10:00 a.m. to continue on. We were all in agreement, but my insides were quivering still not knowing what "like me" meant. The thought of waiting until the next day was almost unbearable. It had been a very long day, and I think we were all emotionally exhausted. Besides, I told myself that it would give me a chance to digest everything that was said up until now and to prepare for the rest of this incredible narrative. Naturally, I was anxious with anticipation, but by now, I had learned to be patient. Go figure!

Chapter 34

Session Four Summary

Sean, Liam, and I were more than fine with calling it a night. We hadn't eaten all day and were hungry. I think we all needed a strong cocktail as much as we needed food. I know I did!

We stopped at one of our favorite places and tried to relax but found it nearly impossible. I couldn't help but move from one thought to another and then another. It was almost too much to comprehend. Sean said, "Now do you understand why Dr. Jill wouldn't give you information in bits and pieces?"

I told Sean that I could definitely see the logic in her decision, but I had to ask them how in the world they were able to keep it to themselves without divulging anything to me. They both said that it wasn't easy, but they knew that Dr. Jill was only interested in my welfare as they were too. We were all still pretty tensed up and needed some breathing room. We placed our order and asked for a second drink. Feeling a little selfish, I realized that our conversation was limited to my situation, but we were all consumed with Dr. Jill's summary of my first three sessions. I knew that I wouldn't have a peaceful sleep that night. I knew I'd be replaying the summaries in my head. I prayed that I would get a little quality rest though as I wanted to be fresh and alert for my next appointment when session number four would be disclosed. I knew that I needed to concentrate on each question and answer in every single tape, but I didn't want to even try to do that while the three of us were together. It's just not the right time. I needed to spend some time alone so that I could process all the information that Dr. Jill shared with me. Although they completely understood my single-minded focus, I apologized and said that we needed to change the subject for a while.

I asked Liam how he was doing as I hadn't seen him since my last session. He acted as if nothing had changed in his life, so it became very apparent that he didn't want to discuss his new love interest with me. His silence told me that I'd better not approach the subject either. He had to know by now that Sean would tell me all about his new friend. I was glad that I hadn't approached him on the subject before.

We always enjoyed being together, so we engaged in idle chat throughout the rest of our meal. By now, I was more than ready to go home. I was so emotionally tired and almost always needed time to unwind before going to bed, but tonight, I had a feeling that I'd be going straight to bed, not necessarily to sleep but to reflect on this newly discovered story about myself. Sean still needed that time and said that he would join me a little later.

The night was indeed much too short, but Sean and I managed to drag ourselves out of bed in time to have coffee and prepare for my 10:00 a.m. appointment. I don't know what I would ever have done without Sean in my life, and I didn't even like thinking about it, but I did find myself thinking about it quite a lot. I honestly can't think of another person who would want to invest so much time and effort in my life and my problems. In an earlier exchange of dialog about my mixed-up bewildering life, he told me that I was heaven-sent. If he had changed his mind about that, he didn't let on. I think he is the one who is heaven-sent, and I thank God for him every day.

Dr. Jill was prepared to continue with her summary, and we wasted no time getting right down to the heart of the matter.

Dr. Jill said, "As you know, the first three sessions were summarized. Before we get started on the forth, since you've had time to think about it, do you have any questions for me?" Oddly enough and much to my surprise, I said that I didn't. The only burning question on my mind was the "like me" question, but I knew that we would eventually be getting to that. One would think that I would have a million questions, but I didn't because I was beginning to see that progressing through each tape would answer most of the questions I had. So much was already making sense of my senseless life.

"If you recall, we left off where you commented on them not being finished with you yet and said that you didn't know why they weren't finished with you yet. I asked you if they were angry with you because of what you thought or if it was because you verbalized your thoughts, and you answered, 'Both.' Most times they would communicate through telepathy, but they would talk to you when you thought they were changing their appearance. At that moment, you were showing agitation and fear because they wanted to go into the private room, and you knew that was never a good sign. You went on to tell me that they were having a discussion among themselves. They were discussing who would go first and arguing about some agreement. You were unable to hear everything and couldn't tell me about the agreement right at that moment. They had made their decision as to who was to go first." Dr. Jill said, "Princess, this next revelation is incredibly hard for me to say, and I know it's going to be even harder for you to hear, but it's important that you know the truth and hear everything."

I assured Dr. Jill that I would be fine and that I didn't want her to leave a single thing out.

Dr. Jill continued on. In their discussion, they were arguing about who would be the first to rape you.

"Wait! What? Rape me?" I looked at Sean, then Liam, and back at Dr. Jill. I couldn't hold back the tears. Sean put his arm around me and pulled me closer to him. So far, I was accepting of the information that Dr. Jill gave, but this, this, is just too much. I then asked Dr. Jill to continue.

"When I asked you how many of them were in the room with you, you indicated that there were four or five. I then asked you what they looked like, and you said, 'Both.' They looked like regular men, but you couldn't identify the others. We finally learned that they are undeniably two separate types of beings, working together. You said that they viewed you as their most frustrating project."

I was still focused on the rape part of the story, so I said, "Dr. Jill, would you mind if we take a little break? That was indeed very hard to hear, and I need a few minutes to digest all this."

Dr. Jill understood perfectly and said that I should take as much time as I needed because I was the only one that she had scheduled for the day. I told Dr. Jill, Sean, and Liam that I needed to be alone for a few minutes. Sean said that he understood, but in my heart, I knew that he thought I was pushing him away and I hated that. He always wanted to comfort me if I needed comforting. I suppose I was in need of comforting, but I needed some time to be alone with my thoughts. All this actually happened to me, and yet, I remembered nothing until I was hypnotized. I don't think there are any words in the English language that could adequately describe what I was feeling. A couple of tears fell, and I wondered how I could possibly go through something like that and not remember a thing. Of course, I knew why I didn't remember, but the reality of my not remembering didn't seem possible. I finally pulled myself together and wiped the tears away before reentering the room where they were sitting, but Dr. Jill wasn't there. I learned that she actually needed some time alone too, and poor Sean looked like he was hurting as much as I was. I think Liam was just trying to analyze every piece of information thrown out there. I know Sean wanted to hug me, so I sat close to him on the sofa so that we could take comfort in each other. When Dr. Jill reentered the room, I told her that I was ready to continue. She knew that I would want to continue but thought better of it due to the subject matter of the last revelation. She thought it would be best if we gave our emotions a rest and said that she wouldn't share any more information until the following day. In reality, I think Dr. Jill felt emotionally exhausted too. It was better that we all start fresh the following morning.

Chapter 35

Session Five Summary

Dr. Jill wanted to be absolutely certain that I was emotionally established and under control. Otherwise, she would not continue. I assured her that I felt secure enough to finish, especially since Sean was by my side. He put one arm around me and held my hand with the other. "Please continue," I said.

Dr. Jill said that she had asked me if the rape took place during the same encounter when they injured my face so badly. I said, "No, it was another time." I told her that Sean and Liam didn't know that I had left and returned because it probably happened over night.

Dr. Jill said that during session five, she addressed the agreement again. She wanted to know more and asked me what I thought the agreement was. She said that for a short time, I thought it was some type of secret government program. After thinking about it, I changed my mind about that. Dr. Jill asked if the agreement was strictly for me. I said that it was for me and others like me and reminded her that I can remember things because I'm different on an intelligence level. Apparently, the agreement had two stipulations, but I was feeling threatened in some way and couldn't say any more at that time. Dr. Jill waited to question me further during sessions six.

After inquiring about my state of mind and comfort level, Dr. Jill proceeded with her summary of session six.

Dr. Jill asked if they had the ability to erase all memories, and I told her that they could, but only for those subjects inclined to remember even the smallest detail of their abduction. They usually didn't find it necessary to do that. She went on to ask why they hadn't removed all my memories, and I told her that they weren't allowed to because of the agreement. They agreed to limit their control and power over people like me. There's that people "like me" thing again. I hope we get to it soon. They were forbidden to have full control and power over people like me. Once again, Dr. Jill then told me that this portion would also be hard to hear but it was the most important detail. It would be another astonishing moment, but it was the detail that tied everything together and couldn't be avoided. She said that she asked me what made me special or different, and I told her that I was a hybrid.

In disbelief, I stopped her. "I'm a what?" I had to ask what a hybrid was.

She said that she was getting to just that, and I should listen to the rest of her summary very carefully. I agreed and she told me that I described a hybrid as being a person with human and nonhuman DNA and that we are considered a valuable experiment. I went on to explain that my mother was human but that I shared many different nonhuman DNAs but I did, however, feel that the most alien DNA within me was Arcturian. Arcturians are intellectually advanced, typically five-feet tall, and greenish in color and have large eyes. Dr. Jill went on to say that I told her that I looked and acted more like a human because the genetics and DNA of my human mother was predominant in my composition and my only alien characteristic was my intellect.

Learning about my lineage has totally blown my mind. I can't wrap my head around this. It's almost too incredible to be true. How could I not know or be aware of such vital information? Once again, the words to describe how I feel totally evade me. Dr. Jill told me to think about everything said about memory and I would have the answer to that question. I couldn't deny that she was right. She said that there wasn't very much left to cover and asked if I wanted her to complete what little was left of session six, and I told her that I did.

She went on to tell me that I couldn't remember who my adoptive parents were but that I knew they were both human and I knew that I was adopted and loved. "You were adopted when you were around age ten and always took advanced classes and some college courses while in high school. After high school, you went on to college but didn't remember the name of the college that you attended or what field of studies you pursued."

Chapter 36

Session Seven Summary

Dr. Jill's questioning in session seven was a continuation of session six, which was typical of each session but was a much shorter session than all the others.

When Dr. Jill asked me where I went to school prior to being adopted, I indicated that I didn't know the name of the school but that I knew that I had attended school with other kids "like me" and that it was a special school for hybrid children. Dr. Jill then asked if all hybrid children went to a special school and if all hybrid children were adopted. Answering her questions, I said that we were all sent to special schools and all hybrid children were adopted, but not all children were adopted later in age. I informed her that some children were adopted as infants if there was nothing special about them. At times, some children don't possess a special talent or increased intellect. After asking if my human parents knew that I was hybrid, I said that they didn't and that they just thought I was really smart.

Dr. Jill said that my sessions had now been concluded and there wouldn't be a need to pursue anything else. She said that she felt that she had covered all the important aspects of the issues surrounding my life. She felt badly and was saddened though by the thought that I would never again know my true identity or where I came from. She wished that there had been another avenue that she could have taken in order to unbury all the hidden and lost memories. As hard as she tried, there was just no way to retrieve that information.

After hearing that there would be no future sessions, I proceeded to thank Dr. Jill for the kindness and patience that she had shown and for helping me to unravel this mystery. It was a huge relief to know what had happened to me and why, but it was still an overwhelming amount of information to process. This was going to take some time, but with Sean by my side and Liam there to support me, I knew that the process would be a little easier.

As we stood up and prepared to leave, Dr. Jill said, "Please don't leave just yet. I have a few more things to tell you." I wondered what more she could possibly have to share. She looked over at Sean, and he immediately knew that she was referring to his session with her. She reminded me that after my seventh session, Sean had asked me to have a seat in the outer waiting room. Sean wanted to express some concerns that he had. I had absolutely no clue.

Sean joined the conversation and said, "Princess, remember when we were playing our game of Scrabble? Well, that wasn't a client calling me. It was Dr. Jill asking me to meet her the following day." Things finally started falling into place. I knew without a doubt that Sean would never be secretive without having a very good reason. His concerns led to his secret meeting with her in an effort to sort things out.

Now, Dr. Jill jumped in to say that she had asked Sean to let her hypnotize him. She needed more answers, and the only way to get them was to hypnotize Sean. My eyes widened, and I stared at Sean in disbelief and said that I was disappointed in him for not sharing that information with me. He looked at Dr. Jill with a hurt look, and Dr. Jill quickly explained that she made it clear to Sean that he was not to say a single word about his visit and also stressed that she didn't share any information about his session. He had no idea what questions were asked, nor did he know how he answered. She felt that what she had learned was of the utmost importance and wanted to share the information with all of us, together. This information would shed a great deal of light on my abrupt appearance that first night.

Dr. Jill was addressing Sean now, "When I hypnotized you, Sean, I asked specific questions about your childhood, schooling, adoption, and your parents. The answers you gave me were almost identical to the answers that Princess gave."

I thought Sean was going to faint! We were all shocked to hear that. After giving Sean ample time to recover, I asked Dr. Jill if there was more to this story, and she indicated that there was. Knowing that Sean was upset, I asked him if he was prepared to hear more or if he needed more time. He indicated that he needed to hear the full story regardless of how unpleasant it might be. I said, "Please go on, Dr. Jill. We need to hear all of it."

Dr. Jill told Sean that when she specifically asked him about his biological parents, he said that he had human and nonhuman DNA. "You said, just as Princess had said, that although you shared many different DNAs, you were more human than anything but the qualities of the Yahyel race stood out. These beings are caring, most kind, and very loving. They have an advanced and harmonious relationship with technology."

Sean needed some serious consoling. He couldn't believe what he had just heard. It was all too much to take in, and he seemed to be beside himself. I guess it was different when I was the subject, but now that he's in the spotlight, he's not so comfortable. I tried to assure him that being a hybrid wasn't horrible. "After all, we have lived with it all our lives and didn't even know it. Growing from childhood, through adolescence, to adulthood didn't seem different in any way. Does knowing that you are a hybrid change the way you feel in your heart or the way you think? Of course, it doesn't. You are still you, and I am still me. The only difference is that you know your name and where you come from." After making that little statement, I looked at Dr. Jill and asked, "Exactly why is that?"

Dr. Jill said that Sean had been completely cooperative with them. There was no need for violence because he never resisted them or remembered anything about his encounters. He had no idea that he had even been abducted. He appeared to be a little calmer now, and Dr. Jill told him to go ahead and ask any questions that he might have. He was so shaken by all this information that he still couldn't speak, at least not for a few minutes. After gaining his composure, he asked Dr. Jill if by chance they touched on the contributions that he made to this project. She said that they hadn't specifically discussed it but confirmed with Sean that he worked in the field of technology. Dr. Jill told him that in this respect, his interest and expertise in technology comes from his nonhuman DNA and that she could only assume that his involvement was connected to technology and hoped that his knowledge would be used for the good of mankind. Then she looked at me and said, "Didn't you tell me that you thought that Sean was the most kind and loving man that you've ever known?" I couldn't deny that I did tell her that. She said, "These are additional characteristics that you share with them Sean. And by the way, Princess, I also think we might have some insight into knowing why you ended up in Sean's apartment that night. It seems that you have a lot in common and what better way for them to keep an eye on both of you at the same time. I don't know if you'll find this as interesting as I do, but in my own mind, I find your entire situation a little ironic too. They found it necessary to be physically abusive to you, Princess, but placed you into Sean's hands, the hands of a loving, caring man that they know will take care of and love you."

Dr. Jill was totally compassionate and understanding. She knew that she had overwhelmed us and said that it was going to take quite some time for us to accept the circumstances of who we are but one day, the thought of it would be as natural as breathing.

Liam, in his usual jovial way, asked Dr. Jill if it was all right for him to ask Sean a question. Dr. Jill assured him that it was perfectly fine. Liam looked over at Sean and said, "Does this mean that we can't be friends anymore, because if it does, this really sucks!"

Then he looked at Dr. Jill and said, "And don't you even think for one minute that I'll ever let you hypnotize me!" Leave it to Liam to lighten the air. Of course, we all laughed, and she told Liam that she had no intention of hypnotizing him, at least not right now!

The guys stood up and shook Dr. Jill's hand, but I gave her a huge hug and told her how profoundly grateful I was that she knew just what to do to help us move on. We finally knew the truth. She told me to contact her any time if I felt the need, and she included Sean and Liam in that invitation.

Chapter 37

The After Party

With our torment behind us and our resolve to come to terms with all of it, we celebrated like never before. I wanted to invite Dr. Jill to dinner, but at the same time, I knew we three needed to be alone right at this particular time. We owed her so much, and I conveyed to them that giving her a simple thank-you felt entirely inadequate. Sean said, "Well, actually, she did get a little more than just a thank-you." I shook my head and agreed that I did know she charged for her services, but as far as I was concerned, her fee could never be too much. I told Sean that we should still plan to take her out to dinner one night to show our gratitude.

We went to a very nice restaurant, had a sumptuous meal, and did way more drinking than we should have. With each new drink order, we couldn't help following the appropriate tradition of raising our glasses with a toast to "health." In our enthusiasm, we started each first sip by saying, "Slainte!" This celebration was the conclusion that we had been waiting for and drinking felt fitting for the occasion. I'm sure that the staff was wondering when we planned to leave, but we had so much to talk about, and I myself found it impossible not to revel in the fact that I needed no further sessions. Maybe it would have been better if we had all gone back to the apartment and ordered carryout. Oh well, it was too late now.

We finally gave in to fatigue and agreed to call it a night. Liam went home, and we crashed the minute we arrived back at the apartment. Being in total comfort now but still wound up, neither of us was ready to sleep. Needing a distraction, Sean turned the TV on, and we watched some silly game show. It did provide us with some form of entertainment for a while. When the wine decided to hit, I knew that bed would be most welcome, and Sean was right there with me. I can't describe the peace that I felt when I laid down that night. While some of the news that I had received about myself was completely disturbing, I knew I had to accept the fact that I would probably be abducted again. And knowing me as I do, I would probably continue to be uncooperative with them, but I also knew that I could handle whatever came my way. With that thought, I drifted off to sleep immediately. I had a peaceful, restful night, but I'm not so sure that Sean did. I already knew, on some level, that I was different, but Sean's world had been totally turned upside down. There was nothing in his life that would seem to indicate that he wasn't as normal as normal could be. He has a lot to come to terms with as do I.

When we woke up the following morning, the air seemed lighter, and the entire atmosphere was more warm and appealing than it ever had been before. It took longer to go through our usual morning routine, but that was only because we still had so much to talk about and quite possibly because we drank too much the night before. I had forgotten what a hangover felt like, but I'm certain that I won't forget again for a long while. Through the headaches, we even talked about us for a little while.

I suddenly remembered that we were planning to visit his parents. I looked over at Sean, apparently with an alarming look on my face, and asked him exactly just how he was planning to explain me. He said that he would try to answer any questions as honestly as possible without revealing too much. I just hope they don't ask for the usual information that most parents want to know. He told me that he was going to have to wing it. I told him that it was all well and good for him, but what if they started asking me questions? He told me to make up a story and stick with it, at least for now. I felt so uncomfortable doing that, but what choice did I have? I wanted to stay as close to the truth as possible without giving anything away. I knew that whatever I decided to tell them, I wouldn't forget the details. After all, I have a great memory.

Sean reminded me that his parents may know that he is a hybrid. I said, "Are you sure about that?" He just stared at me for what seemed like forever and then said that he just didn't know, but giving it more thought, he doubted they even knew what a hybrid was. I mentioned the letter that his parents said they would share with him when the time was right. I told Sean that maybe now the time is right. We discussed it at length and came to the conclusion that we should just play it by ear. We agreed that it might not be wise to bring it up on our first visit there together. I did tell him that he might want to consider asking them about it sooner rather than later though.

Chapter 38

A Time for Thanks

Sean phoned his mum and dad to ask them if the holiday weekend was a good time for a visit. They told him that there was never a bad time and that they were excited beyond words. It had been such a long time since they had gotten together and they had so much catching up to do. Sean thought to himself, *Boy, they're in for a surprise because they don't know the half of it!*

Sean hemmed and hawed a little before he could bring himself to ask if he could bring a special person along with him. Sean's mum said, "A special person? Are you serious? I almost gave up on that thought. I'm so happy for you, Sean. I can hardly wait!" Sean's dad took over the conversation and said that he loved the idea and of course they had two guest rooms and both would be available when we arrived. The first problem was solved in short order. I was going to be welcomed with open arms. They just didn't know what they were welcoming yet. They absolutely loved the idea of Sean having a special friend. Sean and I had a hearty laugh over what his dad had said. I thought that was so sweet and of course funny, but I could understand where he was coming from. I told Sean that if that's the way they wanted it, that's the way it should be and he shouldn't question it.

We didn't know it at the time, but after that telephone call, Sean's parents had a very serious discussion about that mysterious letter still in their possession. It seems that they hadn't forgotten about it at all. Now that there was a special person in Sean's life, they debated back and forth about telling him or not telling him. They decided that if the relationship was serious, they didn't have any right to keep it from him but as parents, they were just as protective of him now as they were when he was a little boy. This unexpected turn of events was more than a little overwhelming for them. They did decide to wait for that right time though. They wanted to be absolutely convinced this special person was "the one."

I was just as excited to meet them as they were to meet me, but I was nervous about it nevertheless. I hated hiding the fact that I didn't know who I was or where I came from, but I didn't have a choice. I couldn't possibly tell them now—not on the first visit. I'd look and sound like a lunatic! We don't even know each other, and they might not take too kindly to Sean having a relationship with me if they knew the truth. I was secretly hoping that they would accept me as Princess for now and be satisfied with that for the time being. I also wanted them to be happy for us, knowing that we were very happy together. I didn't plan to fawn all over him like a school girl, but a little hand holding and an occasional hug seemed to be appropriate. I was, however, very mindful of the fact that they had every right to know about me at some point. I figured that we'd have that discussion with them when the time was right, perhaps when Sean decided the time was right to inquire about the letter.

The days leading up to our departure were typical although Liam dropped by unannounced just like he used to. Things really are back to normal, and we're loving it. Liam shared with us that he had broken off his association with his newest love interest. He said that he felt badly about it because he had special feelings for her and knew in his heart that this relationship could be positive and lasting if she weren't already spoken for. She indicated to Liam that she didn't think her current situation would last, and they agreed that should she become available in the future, they might consider picking up where they left off. We both felt badly for Liam. We knew that his heart was hurting, and we tried to be as supportive as we possibly could be. I found myself trying to find ways to distract Liam instead of myself for a change. We all loved our day out at the arcade, so I suggested that we go to the arcade. They were serious about their jobs, but they seemed to be in their element when they were at the arcade. Both of these little boys perked right up and could hardly wait to leave. I told them to just sit back, relax, and have a beer or something because I was smack-dab in the middle doing something very important and I never liked leaving things unfinished. It was way too early to leave, so I had to make something up, and that sounded as good as anything. I'm so glad that they didn't ask me what I was doing that was so important! I don't think very quickly on my feet, so I'm sure that I probably wouldn't have an acceptable answer.

After watching the two of them pacing around the living room more than I cared to, I said with a smile, "Let's go, guys. I think it's that time." I'm not sure which one of them beat me to the door, but if I hadn't been sandwiched between them, I would probably still be waiting for them to realize that they had forgotten to take me along. This little outing seemed to be just what the doctor ordered. They are both competitive and seemed to love the school boy competition between them for each game they played.

Chapter 39

The Visit

The exciting day finally arrived, and we were off on another adventure. For me, meeting Sean's parents was so important. I felt badly that Sean wouldn't be able to meet mine. As I was thinking about that, a couple of tears slid down my cheek. I was sad that I would never again know who my parents were or about the entire relationship I had with them. I just remember being so loved and growing up in a warm, caring home. Thoughts like this are the exact thoughts that I was finding the most difficult to come to terms with. It seemed so unfair, yet I knew deep down that it was my own fault. If I had been more cooperative, I wouldn't be in this situation. Remembering that there are two sides to every coin, I reminded myself that if I hadn't been uncooperative, I never would have met Sean, and that brought a little comfort to my heart. I turned my head to make it appear that I enjoyed watching the scenery out of my side window. I didn't want Sean to see that I was sad on such a happy day for us. I masterfully concealed my tears and not a moment too soon. We were stopping for gas, excuse me, petrol, and Sean asked me if I minded running into the convenience store to grab a couple of cups of coffee for us. I was more than happy to go inside. It would give me a chance to have a potty break and to splash some water onto my face.

When I returned to the car, I asked Sean how much longer the trip would be until we arrived at our destination. He told me that we were only about an hour and a half out. That made me happy and nervous all at the same time. That hour and a half went by faster than any hour and a half in my life ever had. When we pulled into their driveway, we were met with open arms, hugs, and kisses. Apparently, Sean had phoned them when he was filling the car and told them the approximate time of our arrival. I was greeted as warmly as Sean was, and that gave me such a sense of relief. I've always been able to read people well, and I knew that I was right about them. Their physical touch and my heart told me that their hugs were genuine and sincere. It's so easy to spot insincerity, and I can always tell when a hug isn't heartfelt. I knew that my worries and fears would be few for the rest of our visit. I was stunned to see that neither of them looked like the picture I had created mentally. They both looked so young and were very attractive people. His mum had a slight build and was shorter than me. She had striking auburn hair that rested on her shoulders and framed her face with perfection. I could tell that she was a woman who took care of herself, not in a pampered way but in a healthy way. She obviously took pride in her appearance. His dad on the other hand was a tall, very large, stocky man but also very attractive. He still had a full head of brown hair with some gray sprinkled in here and there and had that same scruffy beard that Sean had. Some time ago, a stubbly face meant that a man just didn't shave, but today, it seems that the rugged look is a positive addition to a man's good looks. I couldn't agree more.

Sitting around the kitchen table was the best and most comfortable place to talk. It was early afternoon, but that didn't stop the guys from enjoying their favorite Guinness. Sean's dad offered me a traditional Irish cream drink, but the original Irish cream drink was much different than the American version. I haven't tasted the original Irish cream drink. I decided that whisky, brown sugar and cream might not be a good choice for now. Sean's mum and I decided on wine for ourselves. I was happy that Sean and his parents were involved in keeping most of the conversation between themselves. I loved just listening to their exchanging stories. I wasn't only learning about Sean's parents; I was learning more about Sean too. At times I found myself inconspicuously surveying the kitchen decor. It was simple but elegant and displayed the utensils of an accomplished cook. Seeing that was a little unnerving and made me question my own skills. At one point, Sean's mum turned to me and said, "Princess, that's an unusual name, but I really like it. It suits you well." I was touched when she said that, and although I wanted to cry when she said those words, I gave her a smile and a thank-you. I told her that I appreciated her kind words. Then she added, "Oh, by the way, you are welcome to call me Mum, and you can call that old coot over there Dad if you want to but only if you are comfortable with that." I told her that I would like that very much. Somehow, she knew just the right words to say. You'd think that she already knew that I would never be seeing my own parents again.

Sean reached over and squeezed my hand as if to say, "See, I told you they were really nice people."

Sean's mum looked over at me and said, "It's time for me to get dinner started."

Sean immediately stopped her and said, "Oh, no you don't. Tonight we are going to order takeout, or Princess and I will be treating you to a dinner out. We have far too much to catch up on."

Sean's dad jumped in and said, "I vote for pizza."

I hadn't thought about pizza since my arrival in Ireland. I guess for some reason, I thought that they wouldn't have pizza in Ireland. I immediately blurted out, "Me too. I haven't had pizza in forever."

Sean's dad looked at me and said, "You're a girl after my own heart!" Sean made a joke of it and told his dad in no uncertain terms that I was his girl and only his girl. His dad said that it was perfectly all right with him because he already had his own girl. Sean's mum and dad absolutely made the sweetest couple. So far, I was feeling incredibly comfortable around his folks. They were my kind of people and as welcoming to me as Sean was when I appeared out of nowhere.

Pizza was delivered, and we had a most enjoyable dinner. They even had some really great wine to go with it. I was thinking that it wouldn't be nearly as good as the pizza I remembered from the states, but I have to admit it, the pizza was pretty good. Being in a new country altogether, I think I expected that it would just be mediocre, but I couldn't have been more wrong. It was almost 10:00 p.m. when we finished cleaning up the kitchen, and I was so tired. It had been a long day, and I thought that the anticipation of meeting Sean's mum and dad for the first time was emotionally exhausting. Even though it was still fairly early, I excused myself and said that I was going to turn in. Sean said that he wasn't going to be far behind me. At that juncture, Sean's dad said that we were welcome to share a room if that's what we wanted to do. Sean just stared at his dad, and his dad said, "What? I'm progressive! Do you think we were born yesterday?"

I gave him a little wink and Sean laughed saying, "Thanks, Dad. You have no idea how grateful I am to know that you are so open-minded." I don't think Sean was thinking only of the bedroom arrangements. He was anticipating the rest of our visit for this trip and looking a little bit forward to the next one. There was still so much more to be told, and we hadn't even started telling our story.

Chapter 40

Day Two with Mum and Dad

Sleeping in must have been the order of the day because we all slept in until late morning. By the time we had showered and readied ourselves for the day, it was almost 11:00 a.m. Still having so much to catch up on, we decided to spend some time around the kitchen table again. It was too late for breakfast, so Mum and I prepared brunch, which didn't take long. We enjoyed our coffee while Sean told his folks about his new client and of course about the new girlfriend that Liam almost had. They know Liam quite well because he was around a lot as a teenager and of course also because of his close friendship with Sean. I think they know Liam almost as well as Sean does.

The way the conversation was going, I could tell that Mum and Dad were nearing a point to where one or the other was going to ask about some of my background. I couldn't blame them, but I have to say that I was feeling frazzled and nervous at the thought of having to come up with some kind of believable story. I hated that feeling because I was not a dishonest person and I didn't want to mislead them. As sure as I was sitting there in the kitchen, she looked over at me and said, "Tell us a little something about you. I feel badly that we have been centering on only us all this time."

I told her that I didn't mind and that I enjoyed hearing all the stories and getting to know them.

She said, "I'm sure you do, but we'd like to get to know you too."

I told them that there wasn't much to tell. I had a very typical childhood. I told them that much like Sean's circumstances, I too had been adopted by wonderful, caring people just like they were.

Sean's mum broke in and said, "I can tell that you're from the United States. Did you move from the states to permanently stay in Ireland? Or did your job perhaps bring you here? You've obviously been here long enough to meet Sean and develop a relationship." I'm not used to being deceptive, and I was about to become undone by her interrogation. I stood up to clear the table, but I found myself nervously moving from side to side with my hands in my pockets.

Sean could see that I was getting uncomfortable and quickly interrupted, taking over the conversation with the first thing that popped into his head. He obviously didn't have a prepared statement, and he must have been nervous too because what he said was the most ridiculous thing I've ever heard. Out of the blue, he nonchalantly said, "Hey, why don't you guys have a dog or a cat? A horse might even be nice." His mum's and dad's eyes got as big as saucers. I thought they were both going to fall off their chairs. If I had been sitting, I know that I would have fallen off mine. His mum stood up and felt his forehead as if he was going to feel feverish.

She said, "What? I can't believe you just asked that. What are you thinking, son?" Sean went on to tell them that the older lady across the hall from us had several cats and he just thought that most elderly people had pets. They were still dumbfounded.

His dad said, "Elderly? You're calling us elderly? I know we're older now, but we aren't exactly dead!"

Sean said, "Good heavens, no, Dad, I'm not implying that you're elderly. I just thought that since you haven't had a kid at home for a while now, you might want to have a pet of some kind." By now, I'm sure they were questioning Sean's sanity. I knew what he was doing, but I had to admit, I was thinking the same thing his mum and dad were thinking for a minute or two. I was so glad that he was able to change the conversation, and he surely did that! There was no doubt about it. It did go into a whole new direction. I was dying inside and found it hard not to laugh out loud. Sean slid his chair out, away from the table, and insisted that we go take a little drive around town. It was easy to see that his folks still thought he was absolutely loony. Knowing Sean as they did, they weren't about to be fooled for very long. They knew he deliberately changed the subject of the conversation and was holding something back, but they didn't push for an explanation. For the time being, they played along with his nonsense. Knowing him as they did, they knew that he would speak up when he was comfortable doing so.

I'm not sure how we made it out the door because it all seemed so bizarre. I looked over at Sean and said, "Don't you think it would be a good idea to ask your mum and dad to join us?" He seemed flustered and almost embarrassed that he hadn't and motioned to them to get into the car, but he still had making our escape his priority. If they were with us, they could still ask questions, but that was a risk that we'd have to take. Hopefully, we could keep them busy telling us about this nice place that they lived. We could only hope. Still somewhat confused, they got into the car. Sean's dad sat up front with Sean, and I sat with his mum in the back. She looked over at me, and her face had questions written all over it. I know she was dying to ask me what was going on, but she didn't dare. She knew Sean would come clean sooner or later. For now, they would have to stay in the dark.

Chapter 41

Third Day with Mum and Dad

Our time with Mum and Dad was far too short, but we knew that we'd be seeing them again soon. Knowing that we would be leaving for home soon, we felt that we should have a brief talk with them. We apologized to them for all the mystery and wanted them to know that their son wasn't totally off his rocker. He was just trying to protect me. Promising them that we would clear the air and tell them everything during our next visit, we asked for their patience a little longer. Even though I wanted to tell them our story right then and there, we didn't have enough time to tell it all from beginning to end. Not only that, but also it just didn't seem like the right time. I'm sure they didn't look forward to having to wait, but they seemed satisfied knowing that they would be hearing the truth soon.

We thanked them for a wonderful weekend and said that we would keep in touch more often, as Sean used to do before he met me.

We said our goodbyes and hugged, and we went on our way. Reliving Sean's crazy moment, we couldn't keep from hysterically laughing. I told him that even though he didn't have a well-thought-out plan, I was grateful that he took over and, if there was a next time, to refrain from insulting the senior citizens.

By the time we got home, we were both exhausted. It seems as though most of our excursions had emotion attached to them. I expected that they would for quite some time. I thought that once we told our story and got everything out in the open, we would be able to rest easier and get on with some normalcy in our lives. All we did was ride in a car for a few hours, but we were tired all the same. We did have a slight delay due to an accident, but it didn't add much time to our travel.

We carried our bags in and changed clothes. I told Sean that I would do the unpacking in the morning. We sat in the living room and watched a little TV. We hadn't watched any news at all while we were gone, so I turned on the news to see if we had missed anything. The news was usually pretty mundane but not tonight. It seems that a young woman was beaten badly and left to die on a sidewalk in town. She was taken to the nearest hospital, but the doctors weren't hopeful about her prognosis. We hardly see news like that locally. Our little corner of the world is basically crime-free. Yes, we do hear of crime but nothing like that. After seeing that, we had seen enough. It's not exactly a good way to end a day. We turned the TV off and called it a day.

We climbed into bed, and because Sean is always so good to me, I hugged him and told him how much I appreciated him. Since ending my sessions with Dr. Jill, there was a new kind of peaceful mood in the atmosphere that we felt every single day. Unlike before, falling asleep was effortless. Sean held me tight, and we were both asleep almost immediately. Even though I'm sure we have a somewhat false sense of security, I think we both feel that I won't be taken again as long as we are holding on to one another.

Morning came without incident. We weren't long into our usual morning routine before Sean's phone rang. It was Liam, and he was talking a hundred miles an hour. Sean told him to slow down and speak slower so that he'd understand what he was actually saying. Liam was a total mess. Sean said that, with the exception of the time I was missing, he's never seen Liam so upset. Sean really did have a lot of work to do but hated to let Liam down. Liam had been Johnny on the spot every time Sean or I needed him. Sean decided that his work would just have to wait awhile longer and asked Liam if he wanted to talk on the phone or in person. Liam wanted to talk in person and told Sean to go to his apartment but then changed his mind and said that he would come here. Sean asked Liam if he was sure that he was in a condition to drive safely. Liam swore to us that he was and that he'd be here shortly.

About twenty minutes later, Liam was at the door. When he came in, noticing that he was a total mess wasn't difficult. His hair wasn't neatly combed as it usually was, and the buttons on the front of his shirt were mismatched with the corresponding button holes. His appearance was alarming as I've never seen him in such a condition. I even checked to see if he had a matching pair of shoes on. I asked him if he wanted me to leave so that he could talk to Sean alone. Liam knew that Sean and I kept no secrets from one another, so he told me to stay. There was no beating around the bush with Liam. He asked if we had heard the news about a young woman being beaten and left for dead on the street. We told him that we did watch the news and heard about it. Liam proceeded to tell us that Hannah was that young woman! She was the woman that he had been seeing. The news didn't mention a name, so we had no way of knowing it was Hannah. He felt guilty and responsible for what had happened to her. He felt sure that her husband found out about them and beat her for it. They certainly didn't have a solid relationship, so the husband was Liam's suspect. He couldn't be 100% positive as the abuser hadn't been found yet, but he felt in his heart of hearts that it was the husband. He said that he hadn't gone to the authorities because he knew that the husband would be the first to be questioned. He was hoping that there would be some physical evidence that the husband was the attacker. If he used his hands to beat her, there would be bruising and trauma to his fists or possibly scratches if she fought back.

I think that just talking to someone about his concerns helped him a great deal. There wasn't much we could say, so we became good listeners. Sean told Liam that he thought it might be a good idea for him to go to the authorities to tell them that he did know this woman. Sean was afraid that Liam would be considered a suspect if the husband wasn't the guilty party. Liam had no signs of physically abusing anyone, and he had to let them see his physical appearance right now. Not showing signs of any kind of struggle, Liam would surely be eliminated as a suspect. If he waited, he would have no way to prove that he had nothing to do with it. The inspectors were sure to find out that the woman was seeing someone outside of her marriage and they had their ways of finding out who that was. Liam agreed and asked Sean to go with him. We all prayed that she would pull through and identify her attacker, but given her condition, we didn't know if that would be the case.

Sean accompanied Liam to talk to the authorities, which didn't seem to take very long. They photographed Liam's hands, arms, neck, and face to add to the official file, and then Liam told them his story. The authorities couldn't share any information with him at this point in the investigation, so all he could do was hope that he wasn't implicated in any way.

Chapter 42

False Alarm

With the exception of Liam's uncertainty about his future, the following weeks were as normal as they could be. Sean was caught up on work, and I tended to my self-assigned duties around the apartment.

Thankfully, we just found out that Hannah, the young woman who had been so badly beaten, was improving every day. For her protection, the inspector placed an around-the-clock guard outside her hospital room. He felt that she would be identifying her attacker very soon and didn't want her to be in any potential danger. Her attacker might not like hearing that she survived. We were all anxious to hear her story. At this point, they hadn't even allowed her husband to visit her, not even with supervision. They weren't taking any chances. Liam was relieved to hear that because it meant that they did indeed consider him a suspect.

Sean and I did what we usually do, mirroring the activities of the day before if we didn't have any new plans. I did make that effort to get to know Mrs. MacDonald better. She is such a sweet lady. I'm usually not a procrastinator, but our lives have been so topsy-turvy and hectic since my arrival here. I felt badly that I hadn't taken the time to get to know her better by now. Liam was experiencing so much anxiety that he was a full-time job there for a while. I decided that it was time to invite Mrs. MacDonald to our apartment one afternoon. She is a tea drinker, and Sean had noticed the brand that she liked sitting on her kitchen counter during one of his helpful visits. I made sure that I had the kind of tea that she liked. We actually talked for quite some time, and I found her to be fascinating. She is the sweetest little lady. When she smiles, the deep dimples in her cheeks make her look so angelic, and every hair was neatly combed into place. Now, when I think of her, I'll be comparing her to one of those chubby little cherubs. She's quite the talker too. When she tells me one of her many stories, she inserts the most picturesque speech, and I get lost in my own imagination. I can't say that I blame her for being a talker though. Spending so much time alone with only her cats to converse with, I'm sure she has a lot to say. She told me about herself and of course her husband starting from the day they were married. She was married at the age of eighteen in the year 1950. Mr. MacDonald was born and raised in County Cork, so that's where they took up residency. Though they tried to have a family, they were never blessed with a child. With love in her eyes, she leaned in as if what she was about to say was a secret and quietly confided that Sean was very special to her. She viewed him as the son she never had. Adopting a child was a consideration, but they decided not to follow through with that pursuit. She didn't say why, so I didn't pry into something so personal. She would quickly move on from one subject to the next almost without taking a breath. She quickly interjected the fact that County Cork was not part of the United Kingdom. Occasionally, when she did stop for a breath, she would gaze off into space, and I could tell that she was reliving a special time that she had experienced. I could never tell if she was thinking about a time prior to being married or if she was thinking about an adventure that she and Mr. MacDonald had. She would usually tell me the story that was circling her head but not always. Some things are just too precious to share and should be kept in that secret place in the heart. Her life was extremely interesting, and I found that I wanted to know more and more. As time passed, I learned so many new things about her and also about County Cork. Some of the information that she shared made so much sense. Now I get it! I could never figure out why Sean was so keen on eating out so much. As I was finding out, it wasn't because of my cooking but because he was raised here in Ireland's Foodie Capital, the culinary capital of Ireland. Here, people are encouraged to eat a lot! I'm surprised that I haven't seen more obese people here than I have, and now I can see why Mrs. MacDonald is a little plump. It's not just from her cookies. Mrs. MacDonald truly appreciated that I had taken an interest in her, and we became quite good friends, meeting at least once a week to visit over a cup or two of tea. At one point, she told me that we had been friends long enough to be on a first-name basis. She has always called me Princess, but now I was expected to call her Imelda. I love her beautiful name, but I can't help but feel a little uncomfortable calling her by her first name. Calling her anything but Mrs. MacDonald almost seems disrespectful. On the other hand, I don't want to hurt her feelings either.

Today, Sean phoned his mum and dad just to check in with them and make sure that they were both well. Sean's mum wanted to talk to me, and we had the nicest chat. We didn't talk about anything personal or special, just generalities. She talked longer to me than she did with Sean, and I thought his nose was a little out of joint. It didn't last long though. He was very glad to see that we got on so well, and we both looked forward to our next visit.

That night, Liam called and wanted Sean to meet him for a beer. He was feeling much better about everything and just wanted some company for a little while. I didn't mind because I had started reading another good romance novel and I was looking forward to picking up where I left off. My reading didn't last too terribly long though. I was so tired that I was in bed before Sean got home. I didn't even hear him come in.

The next morning, I woke up really early, I'm sure because I was in bed and asleep much earlier than usual. I didn't want to disturb Sean because I had no idea what time he had wandered in the night before. I carefully slid out of bed, tiptoed out of the room, and closed the door. I quietly made a big pot of coffee and sat at the kitchen table reading more of my book and sipping on that wonderful morning pick-me-up from my mug. All of a sudden, Sean came running out of the bedroom, down the hall, and into the living room screaming my name the whole time. I ran out of the kitchen, and he was standing there, nearly in tears with hands over his eyes. I screamed that I was right there and asked him what was wrong. He ran over to me and hugged me so tight I thought he was going to break my ribs. He said, "I thought they took you again. When I woke up and found that you weren't there by my side, I thought the worst." Thank God, that wasn't the case. He said, "Don't ever do that again! You scared me to death." I promised him right then and there that if I was the first to get up, I would make absolutely sure that I informed him by leaving a note on my pillow. That way, his sleep wouldn't be interrupted.

He joined me in the kitchen, and I poured him a cup of coffee. He was still out of breath, and his hands were a little shaky. I hugged him and told him to calm down and take a deep breath. It's such a good feeling to know that I can comfort him for a change. I was absolutely fine, and to my knowledge, I hadn't had any new encounters with them. If I had, I didn't remember it. All I know is that I haven't endured their wrath in a very long time.

That afternoon, Liam phoned Sean to let him know that Hannah's husband was indeed Hannah's attacker and had been arrested. There was no question about his being the attacker. It seems that the young woman was well enough to identify him, and it looked like she was going to be fine. She had a lot of healing to do, but she would be fine.

Sean and I made plans to visit his mum and dad again. We didn't think it would be fair for us to keep them wondering about his strange behavior any longer. Even though we were sure that they didn't think he was totally nutty, it was time to tell them everything. We didn't know where we were going to begin, but we always seem to figure things out, even if it's accidentally.

Chapter 43

Disclosure

During Sean's last phone conversation with his mum, they talked about making plans for our next visit. His mum suggested over the Thanksgiving holiday. It would be such a nice time for family to be together. From what I understand, Thanksgiving isn't a national holiday in Ireland. But Sean's mum told him that she sensed that I needed to feel a place of belonging and thought that celebrating Thanksgiving in November, as we normally would in the states, might give me a little feeling of being home. She was so tuned in to what other people were feeling. I couldn't help but wonder if she is perhaps an empath and is a very special person in her own right. I would soon be having the opportunity to learn more about them and the Irish family traditions that they shared as well.

When we arrived, they greeted us with their usual warmth and a big Happy Thanksgiving. I couldn't begin to express the new feelings that I was experiencing. I felt in my heart that I was going to be an important part of a special family.

Mum had planned a huge American celebration meal with all the fixings. She didn't leave a single item of food out, and I was fortunate enough to be there to help her prepare it. We had great fun in the kitchen, and I learned some of her cooking techniques. She is impressive in the kitchen and is a darn good cook, and I found out that I still have a lot to learn. My cooking hasn't killed Sean yet, but I would like to be as good a cook as his mum is. In the meantime, we all thoroughly enjoyed her wonderfully planned traditional Thanksgiving meal, but we didn't dine on the traditional American pumpkin pie for dessert. Instead, dessert was reserved for a traditional Irish apple crumble. It was a melt in your mouth treat and was Sean's favorite.

The first two days of our visit were spent on catching up. We weren't able to see them often enough and always had so much news to share with them. On the third day, we told them that we needed to sit and talk with them about something truly important. Sean's mum looked relieved that Sean was finally going to come clean. They agreed and said that they had been patient for a long time and were more than ready to hear our story and more than anxious to get rid of the cloud of concern held over them for far too long. Before we even started, Mum blurted out, "No, Sean, we don't have a dog, a cat, or a horse." She said, "See, Sean, I do have a sense of humor." Holding the laughter back was impossible.

We met in their sitting room where the overstuffed furniture offered way more comfort than we needed after such a huge meal. Sean told his parents, "First, before we start telling you our story, I have to ask you about something that I recently remembered hearing as a child. At least, I think I remember hearing it. On the day that my adoption was finalized, did you tell me that you were given a letter that you were to share with me at the right time?"

Sean's mum said that his recollection was correct.

Sean went on to say, "Mum, Dad, I think that this might be the right time. If I'm right, it will become part of the story that we're about to tell you." Sean's mum looked over at his dad and gave a nod of approval. They too sensed that this was indeed the right time. Sean's dad walked into their bedroom and returned with the perfectly preserved letter. The envelope was still sealed and had yellowed a little with age. Sean carefully opened the envelope and removed the letter. The creases were firmly set, and opening it proved to be a little unnerving. He didn't want to damage it in any way. He began reading the lengthy letter out loud so that we would all have the benefit of hearing the account in this mysterious journal.

"My dearest son, I can only assume that you are about to have a very important conversation with your mum and dad. I hope I'm right in that assumption because what I am about to say will probably shock them if they haven't yet figured it out on their own.

"Your adoptive parents have no way of knowing what is written here. They were asked to keep this letter sealed and to allow you to read its secrets only when the time was right. I trusted that they would know when that right time comes.

"I'm going to start at the very beginning. I have a tendency to wander at times, but I'll try to be direct and to the point. When I was a young woman, I found out that I was pregnant. Very early in my pregnancy, I was abducted like so many other young women were. During the abduction, alien DNA was introduced into your body, and you were to be considered a hybrid child."

Sean glanced up at his mum and then at his dad. He could tell by their demeanor that they had no idea what a hybrid child was. He continued reading. "There were even times when mothers would awaken to find that they were no longer pregnant. It was then that babies were taken away in order to develop in an artificial environment somewhere among the alien population. At other times, as was the case in my pregnancy, I was allowed to carry you to full term and give birth to you. I use the term 'allowed' because I knew that once you were born, I was expected to give you up. Because I had no husband and no means by which to support you properly, I didn't see that I had much choice, so I agreed just as they had planned. I found out later that unmarried women were usually chosen to fulfill their program because they were usually easy to manipulate. Because they were aware of the human emotion called love, they needed women who felt that they had no choice but to give up their babies for the good of the child. These beings are completely void of emotion of any kind but knew that we human mothers would go to the ends of the earth to keep and protect our babies if at all possible. I knew that I couldn't provide for you, and giving you up was the hardest thing

I've ever done. I literally thought my heart was breaking into tiny pieces that could never be mended.

"When you were born, it was a time when we specially chosen mothers were allowed to watch our children grow and develop from a distance. I was allowed to watch you from that distance until your initial schooling and adoption were finalized. It wasn't easy for me, but I loved you more than life itself. My heart physically ached knowing that I could never touch you, hold you, kiss your cheek, or whisper that I loved you. In my heart though, I knew that making the decision that I made was in your best interest, and I wanted you to come first, before anyone or anything. If you knew nothing else in your life, it was my greatest desire that you be happy and loved.

"I was also fortunate enough to have a say in your future, and you need to know that I am the one who chose your adoptive parents. I studied every aspect of their lives and knew in my heart that they were people of great integrity and loved each other very much. That's why I was sure that they would honor my wishes. You were carefully placed into the hands of two breathtakingly beautiful souls. They possess every quality that I felt was important and would be the perfect parents to protect you and teach you everything you would need to know in order to navigate through life, but most importantly, I knew that they would love you as I do.

"While I'm not at liberty to reveal any personal details about myself, at least, you know our story. You must know by now that you are very special and why. We are all so very proud that you have become the person that you are. I am especially proud to be a part of you and you a part of me.

"I know that you've grown into a fine young man, and I pray that you have found that special someone to share your life with. If you have found that special someone, I know she is sitting beside you right now and sharing not only your newfound knowledge but your life as well. I also knew that you wouldn't choose just anyone. How I wish I could meet her. I know that she is as special as you are.

"By now, you're probably wondering why I was allowed to write this letter.

"The truth is, since giving birth to you, I've been relentless in my pursuits, and I continually approached the powers that be for approval until they finally gave in and said yes, I think just to quiet me. Actually, that did surprise me as we both know what they are capable of. They aren't particularly fond of being told what to do and how it's going to be done.

"In closing, please know in your heart that I will continue loving you until my dying day, as will your adoptive parents. I am eternally grateful to them for always being the parents that I knew they would be.

"I wrote this letter because of my own selfish need for closure, but I hope, in some way, that I have filled in some of the missing pieces for you. When you have finished reading this, I hope that you will place the letter back into the envelope and gently hold it to your chest, for when you do, I'll feel it in my heart and soul and I'll know that my mission has been completed. I will carry you in my heart forever. I love you.

Your other mum."

We all sat there quietly for a minute as Sean returned the letter to the envelope and pressed it against his chest for several seconds. Our heads were bent as though we were in prayer and playing a role in honoring her wishes. Sean stood up, gave each of us a hug, and expressed his love and appreciation for endless support with love and encouragement for all of his endeavors.

Sean told his mum and dad that we were aware of the fact that he was a hybrid child but couldn't go into detail about that yet. There was so much more to the story leading up to his acquiring this knowledge, and that story began with me, his Princess. They looked at each other totally baffled and confused. How could Sean's story possibly involve me? They were about to find out.

Chapter 44

An Irish Blessing

Starting at the very beginning, we told them the entire account of my appearing out of nowhere and even of the condition I was in. The more information that we gave them, the more I could see their eagerness to learn more and the sadness in their eyes as we told our story that let me know that they were people who felt emotion very deeply. But they were definitely out of their comfort zone. While they were of course interested in hearing more about Sean's being a hybrid, at this particular moment in time, for some reason, they seemed fixed on learning more about me. Sean's mum stood up from her chair and moved forward until she was standing in front of me. Kneeling down and gently taking my hands into hers, she looked up with tears streaming down her face. It was as if her heart and soul actually felt what I had gone through. I didn't even know that I was still carrying a heavy burden with such an enormous weight resting on my shoulders, but when she looked into my eyes, it was as if she unlocked a new door to my heart, and it became so light and open. The added weight was lifted, and I was left speechless. It's impossible to explain. Although words weren't needed, she said, "I love you, Princess," and gave me a hug. I think his dad wanted to do the same thing, but he was too emotional to speak and words didn't come as easily to him as they did to mum. At that point, there was nothing left to tell. His mum and dad still needed to be filled in with the rest of our very long journey by listening to the seven tapes. Knowing what they now know about Sean helped to open the door to the next part of our journey. Hearing the actual tapes was the only way for his mum and dad to fully appreciate the events that took place, and they would explain our past vagueness and our search for the truth.

Now that Sean and I had set the groundwork by telling them about my showing up out of nowhere and about my injuries, it was time for them to continue on with our journey. We tried not to leave out a single detail and filled in as many pieces as we could up until my first hypnosis session with Dr. Jill. From there, Sean suggested that they listen to every tape for themselves knowing that they would have a better understanding of the disturbances ruling our lives for several months. Knowing that it would take some time to listen to all the tapes, we thought it best to let them listen in private at their leisure, starting with tape number one. We are all too aware of the amount of information contained in these tapes and what it takes to absorb it all. I told Sean that I hoped they were in good health so the shock of all this wouldn't be too much for them to handle. He expressed the same concern, but he knew that this was the only way to give them what they had been waiting for. To give them anything less wouldn't be fair to them.

We didn't want to be a distraction, so we thought it best to make ourselves scarce. Any questions that they might have can be answered later. Since there were seven tapes to listen to, in all likelihood, this would become at the very least a two-day experience. We gave them the privacy that they would need and went into another part of the house. I asked Sean if his mum and dad had photo albums of their family during his childhood. He said, "Sure, they do. As you can tell, they didn't hide me in the closet for twenty some years!" I could hardly stop laughing at the picture he had just painted. Sean located the albums, and we spent hours looking through them. At one point, I couldn't help but notice a basket sitting on the floor by the chair. When I looked inside, I found a gorgeous needle point that Mum was working on. She had almost completed it, and there was only a small portion left to finish. I can see that this is another one of her skills I'm hoping to learn. I was secretly hoping that she would offer it to me when she was finished. It was a beautiful Irish blessing. While there are many Irish blessings, to me, this was the best and my favorite. "May the road rise to meet you, may the wind always be at your back, may the sun shine warmth upon your face, may the rains fall softly upon your fields, and until we meet again, may God hold you in the palm of his hands." That blessing doesn't leave a single sentiment out. Mum only had to complete the last line, and her project would be finished. I pictured the perfect frame and the perfect place to display it in our apartment. Concentrating on the photos again, Sean said that he knew most of the people in them but there were a few people that he didn't know. They were probably friends or associates of his folks. He looked at me and said, "I think they'll be starting a new album now, and you'll be in some picture on every page." What a wonderful thought that was because it let me know that this was absolutely my family now and Sean truly wanted to keep building our relationship.

Several hours had passed, and it was getting late. We hadn't given any thought to food, but the Thanksgiving leftovers were calling out to us. We snuck into the kitchen to begin warming up our meal. We prepared enough to cover all four of us because we knew that they hadn't taken a break from the tapes and they would want to eat too. As we were placing everything on the table, Sean's mum and dad walked into the kitchen. Luckily, they had just finished listening to one of the tapes and could smell the warming food. They were just as hungry as we were.

We talked while we were eating, but the atmosphere had changed drastically. The air was heavy and filled with a melancholy that seemed to follow Mum and Dad when they entered the kitchen. To lighten the mood, Sean touched on a new subject. He asked his mum to tell me about their wedding. It was unique in that Irish weddings involve the holding of hands with someone else tying a ribbon around their wrists to bind their union. This was referred to as "tying the knot." Mum and Dad weren't too keen on changing the subject, but Sean kept trying and continued his little dissertation explaining to me that the phrase "tie the knot" comes from a wedding tradition that's ancient. It's called the handfasting ceremony. This Celtic prac- tice literally bonds couples together in matrimony by tying knots of cloth around their hands, and two become one. I wondered if I was supposed to be reading between the lines. I momentarily thought that it was quite strange that he picked that subject. The mood still hadn't changed. We finished eating and started to tidy up the kitchen when Mum and Dad walked over to me and hugged me as I've never been hugged before, not even by Sean if you can believe that. They had listened to four tapes. Tears flooded their eyes, and they expressed their disbelief and extreme heartache because of what I had gone through. Just like everyone else, they couldn't imagine such behavior and abuse like that set upon any human being. I actually feared that the final three tapes might put them over the edge. I tried to comfort them by letting them know that I was totally fine and had been for quite a while and that Sean was the one responsible for helping me to maintain my sanity. I told them that I could never have made it through this ordeal without him and reminded them and myself that what we humans can endure is astonishing. It was obvious now Sean is the love of my life. I was actually grateful to whomever or whatever brought us together, notwithstanding the circumstances. I could tell that we would all be spending much more time together and that our relationship with each other would be long and lasting. We hadn't planned to do much that evening. The mood didn't seem quite right for playing a board game or cards. Sean turned on the TV, and fortunately, he found a movie that just happened to be a comedy. We watched and laughed, but Mum and Dad seemed to be so distracted and miles away at times. They still seemed so sad and disturbed by the first four tapes. I can understand that, but now I wondered if it was wise to let them hear the last three tapes. Still, they needed to know that it was necessary for Sean to be hypnotized too and that he played a huge role in solving the mystery that we didn't even know he played a part in. It took a while for me to regain my composure after hearing the tapes for the first time too, but I'm the one living this nightmare. It's a little different when you're coming into the situation totally cold and unaware that such a thing is even possible. Regardless of anything I would say to lighten the mood, nothing worked.

The following morning, Mum and Dad looked worn-out and drained but said that they were anxious to hear the other tapes. Sean and I told them that they shouldn't feel an obligation to listen to more if it made them feel uncomfortable. Sean's dad said that they needed to hear the full story regardless of how it made them feel. They truly wanted to know every single detail. Before resuming the task of listening to the last three tapes, Mum tenderly asked if I would mind showing her my back. I was totally caught off guard as I wasn't expecting either of them to ask about that, but I had no objection to sharing everything with them. As we stood in their sitting room, Mum slowly lifted my shirt. I don't think that she was prepared to see the real remnants of my injuries. Neither of them expected to see so many telltale signs of abuse. She put her hand over her mouth and took a deep breath. The sight of my back rendered them speechless. I told her that I was grateful that it was only on my back. Clothing can easily cover it, and hopefully with time, the evidence would fade as most scars do. Again, we gave them the time they needed to listen to and digest the information of the remaining tapes.

Chapter 45

Whispers, Warm Feelings and Memories

Sean and I left the house to take in some of the sights of the beautiful community that his parents chose to live in. This was the perfect time to discuss that beautiful letter from his other mum, and I could tell that Sean was thinking about it as well. It was so genuine and honest. I envied Sean and was secretly jealous and feeling sorry for myself because I was deprived of the privilege of hearing the same heartfelt words from my own biological mother. I couldn't help but wonder if my circumstances were the same. To make it even worse, I can't even remember my adoptive parents. The injustice was difficult for me to accept, but what choice did I have? I had to push any negative thoughts out of my head and just be happy for Sean. I was thankful that I was that special someone in his life that his mother talked about. When his other mum said that she knew that I would be as special as he was, it almost seemed as though she had some special insight into his future. I wonder.

By now, Sean's folks would likely be finished with the other tapes. We took the long way back to their house just to give them a few more minutes. When we got back to the house, we saw them standing on the driveway, waiting for us to return. We could see that Mum had been crying again or still. I'm not sure which. She was quiet and distant, and her eyes were swollen and red. She looked up at both of us but then turned her attention to me and said that she couldn't begin to envision how I ever endured that torment for so many months. That would be enough to drive any sane person mad. She put her arms around me and asked if there was anything that she or Dad could do for me. Even though they were more than interested in Sean's hypnosis session, they didn't focus their attention on him. Hearing that he too was a hybrid seemed shocking to them but didn't seem to be the most pressing subject to them. Possibly it was because he didn't suffer physical abuse. They always knew that he was special. They just didn't know how special. I tried to convince her that I was at peace with everything now because having the answers that we had searched so long for made it possible. Sean was at peace too, and all we can do is live every day as it comes. I am comfortable with my new life, and I'm resigned to the fact that a very personal part of my life will remain forgotten forever. While I'm still saddened by that thought occasionally, in all sincerity, I couldn't possibly ask for more than I have right now. All humans experience tragedy of some kind in their lives at some point. Ours was just a little more unbelievable and serious in nature, but we got through it because we had each other for support. We both relied on Liam too at times, and we will forever be grateful to him for being such a faithful friend. I told her that without Dr. Jill, none of us would be living lives anywhere near normal and she is to be applauded for her skill and relentless pursuit of the truth. I gave Mum a hug and told her there was no need for concern or worry. I wanted her to believe in her heart that I accept things as they are now and how grateful I am to have them and Sean in my life. If I do experience another encounter, I'll deal with it when it happens. I can't sit around anticipating when that might be. Thoughts like that would keep us from living. I am truly blessed and very happy. After having said all that, I finally got a smile out of her. I took her by the hand and motioned for the men to follow us into the house. Going straight to the kitchen, I took four wine glasses from the china hutch and filled them, and we toasted to new beginnings. I thought this was an important thing to do as a family unit. Mum and Dad needed to know that nothing would ever be withheld from them again. If a new event is experienced, we will make sure that they know about it. If we needed their help, we will feel free to ask. Mum and Dad have now become part of our crazy, mixed-up story. There isn't much more we can do to put their minds at ease. That will come with time just as it has for Sean and me.

Sean and I realized that our love and respect for each other would keep growing every single day, as it has been. That unusual special connection that we have been sharing has become something beautiful between just the two of us. We are connected in a way that few people have the ability to understand.

I think that having so much drama in our lives has made us stronger than most, and we are living each day as it comes, just one at a time. This journey isn't just a short trip. It's going to last a life-time, and the road that is filled with our footprints will have no end as long as we are still breathing. I dream of spending the rest of my life with Sean and living through the good and bad together, for as long as God allows. Being a realist, I know that not all stories end happily, but I feel like I'm the original eternal optimist. Sean and I have made so many of our own memories, but the memory of that single red rose haunts me and will have a special place in my heart forever because it was the very first official sign of Sean's affection and he really went out of his way to show me that he loved me. While my mind still wanders back to try to capture a part of my previous life, I recall so few things, but I am reminded of a poem that I was drawn to from long ago that felt special to me, and it is called, "Little Rose." Because I had forgotten so much about my life, I was happy to find the entire verse still in my memory bank. Having alien DNA does have its perks once in a while.

I sat there whispering each verse to myself, delighting in warm feelings and memories, especially since I had so few memories left. I thought I was alone when all of a sudden, I felt two hands on my shoulders. I was immediately startled but found that it was Mum. She apologized and walked to the chair that was directly opposite me and sat down. When she looked at me, I could see that her eyes were glistening, but she wasn't exactly crying. I asked her if something was wrong, but she assured me that there was absolutely nothing wrong; and she was fine and said, "Please recite the poem again, but this time, don't whisper the words." I did as she asked, and when I had finished, she was curious to know where I had seen that poem and asked if I knew who the author was. I told her that I did remember reading it in a book of poetry, but the author was nameless. The only word at the end was the word *anonymous*. She seemed unusually interested in it, but when I asked her about it, she said that it didn't have any special meaning. She said, "I just think it's one of the most beautiful things I've ever heard." Even though she tried so hard to give the impression that she was just curious, I felt that there was more to it than she was willing to let on. Since first meeting her, she has always been happy to share everything with me, but she seemed reluctant to share with me now. Why? Why did this poem strike a nerve in her that was undeniable no matter how hard she tried to hide it? I decided not to even try to analyze the situation at that moment, but I knew that I would be giving it much thought over the next few weeks or months.

After reciting it for the second time out loud, I couldn't help but wonder if perhaps there was a reason that I memorized it so long ago. As I repeated the words over and over, they seemed to be more significant than ever. I wondered if those words would somehow become a meaningful part of our lives. It hardly seems fitting to keep it to myself.

Little Rose

She trembled as she held the book
With years of love inside
There, pressed between two pages
Was a flower that had died
She touched it with her fingertips
As the book began to close
This precious tiny gift of love
Her lovely little rose.

If tears could bring it back to life
this rose of ruby red;
her tears would fall so endlessly
she'd cry for him instead.
But there her little rose will stay
for there it's meant to rest;
Of all the gifts he gave to her
She loves her rose the best.

Its petals once were soft and small
It stood tall in the vase,
Though time has changed the way it looks
It just can't be replaced.
It's parched and dry
Yet beautiful
A treasure to behold
She couldn't love it any more
If it were made of gold

Although he left her all alone
He keeps her company
He visits her in memories
That's just as it should be
And in a very special place
She's the only one who knows
Where she keeps her gift of love
Her lovely little rose.

Who knows, perhaps I might even consider writing a book about our
journey one day.

About the Author

Robin was born and raised in a small farming community by the name of Momence, Illinois, and now resides in Henderson, Nevada. Today, she is best known as Mom and Nana. She has enjoyed a variety of interests over the years as well as her job as a legal assistant for over thirteen years until retirement. Having a full-time job and living on a hobby farm at the same time was demanding, but she took pleasure in homemaking, the apple orchard, and of course the company of a husband, a dog, many barn cats, and her true passion, horses.

When her children were little, she found that writing poetry whenever she could was a not only fun but also fulfilling hobby. Being a mom was also demanding, but rewarding beyond measure for her. Now, in her retirement, she decided to take up writing again. But instead of writing poetry, she found a book hiding inside. Discovering that the potential of an untapped imagination is highly underrated, she accepted the challenge. That's when *Princess* was born. In her opinion, first attempts at anything can be awkward, and writing this book was no exception. She thoroughly enjoyed writing *Princess* and took great pleasure in the journey even if the destination is yet to be determined.

CPSIA information can be obtained
at www.ICGtesting.com
Printed in the USA
BVHW081514260123
657211BV00006B/75